STRIPES

BY BRIAN GATTO

SEVEREDPRESS

STRIPES

Copyright © 2024 by Brian Gatto

WWW.SEVEREDPRESS.COM

ISBN: 978-1-923165-17-5

CHAPTER ONE

It swam.

Twenty inches of sinister dorsal fin glided through the water. A triangular-shaped force that had water flowing past it as the beast attached lurked below. The jaws opened and closed periodically to allow water to pass through its gills, a natural filtration. Cycling through the slits on its gills, the act was one of the many impressive features that allowed the fish to survive and thrive. The constant need to push itself forward by swaying its caudal tail back and forth, side to side, was a necessity to life, but that mere fact did not deter it from its function for surviving. To eat and procreate.

With a slight change in direction, the impossibly massive, thirty-two-foot tiger shark glided in a one hundred eighty-degree turn. It faced northwest now and began towards a nearby shoreline. There was splashing about. Its sensory organs picked up the familiar scent of human aromas. Blood was in abundance, everything in the sea bled. This smell was different though. It was contained, as if concentrated in one area.

A mighty sweep of its crescent tail caused sand and small rocks to kick up on the ocean floor. It knocked into a small coral reef, breaking off the top of the foundation. Parts of it hit the bottom with a muffled thudding sound, almost compressed and amplified at the same time.

Its massive girth was evident by the moon above. The orbiting circular rock cast rays of light that shown through the water with a harmless haze. Shadows danced on the skin of the fish like bright waves. Eyes as black and soulless as a button barely moved for they did not search for prey. Sensitive electroreceptors picked up on the cloud of fish chunks and blood.

There were slight splashing sounds that its sensory receptors also picked up on. There were certain attributes that intrigued it. They were small splashes, not too dissimilar to a fish jumping out of the water only to plummet back in with a softening push of the sea.

Ever-growing intrigue brought the shark's attention closer and closer to the source of the smell. Its nose popped out of the water occasionally as if to sniff the night air.

Ahead, a small, rickety fishing boat sat with a man chumming the waters from the stern.

Rocketing forward like a tank, the shark charged for the man on the boat.

Then the screen went black.

"What the hell?" A man of thirty-five years of age stood up from his metal fold out chair.

He quickly ejected the tape from the VCR and inspected it. The paper on it read THE STRIPED DEMON. Everything seemed fine with it. He then reinserted the VHS back into the player, but the screen remained black.

Reaching down for the remote, he found that it was not there. He spun around to see another man standing by the door.

"Loco, what're you doing?" the man asked his confused friend. "The shop's been open for an hour and you haven't even left the office."

"I was watching something," Loco replied, evidence of anger brewing from his scowl.

"Look, I need you to be out on the floor. We need to make sales this week or we'll both be collecting welfare."

"And lose our spot in the mall? Give me a break, Arnold. There are so many better locations to have our venue."

"It's not a venue, it's a gun store. We are a legit business, not some small-time dealer who sells their stock under a tent at a fair." Arnold pressed his head against his temple and rubbed it.

"Head still botherin' ya?"

"You're no help."

"Harsh." Loco got up and began towards the door.

Arnold reached down the chair. "And make sure you push in your chair, for the thousandth time!"

On the sales floor of *Crazy Caliber* stood a regular customer. Both men struggled to remember his name or his occupation. Every morning, they were told but neither cared enough to hear the long, droning tales of retail work and how much it ruins his days. Everything was always a problem with him.

Today was different though. The man appeared more cheerful than usual.

As Loco exited the back room, he cornered him. "Did ya hear the news?"

"Mornin'," Loco sighed.

"What news?" Arnold said as he shut the stockroom door.

"Ginny Darlin!"

"Who?" Arnold inquired.

"A model from this area. She and a crew are heading to Mexico for a photoshoot!"

"A Texan woman wants to cross the border and get pictures taken of her?" Loco chuckled. "And they call me crazy. Doesn't anyone know we have perfectly fine beaches in Texas?"

"I dunno. I'm just spreading the news." The man giggled like a creep.

"Maybe she'll run into the striped demon?" Arnold chuckled.

"Who wha'?"

"It's just a tape Loco here was watching. Some movie about a big ol' shark."

"It's based on a true story. A shark bigger than a truck, longer than a yacht, swims off the coastline."

"Based? More like inspired by a myth," Arnold scoffed.

"So, Ginny will be alright?" the customer asked.

Both Arnold and Loco looked at each other.

"I'm sure your calendar model will be fine," Arnold laughed.

"If not, it'll make for one hell of a photoshoot!" Loco bellowed.

***

It flew, soaring over the Caribbean Sea with a distinguished presence. The aircraft may have been on the smaller end, more akin to a private jet, yet it still held its purpose. Inside were four passengers. They were all eager for the plane to land. With a hint of a downward dip, Josh Rove nearly exclaimed that they were about to arrive. He relaxed himself, awaiting the pilot to announce their status. After a few minutes passed and the intercom remained silent, he sighed.

"We've got to be close!"

"Chillax, man," the man sitting behind him said. "We should be there in twenty or so."

"Twenty or so what, Jackson? Hours? Days? It's taking forever!"

The man Josh referred to was Maurice Jackson, his director. Sitting next to him was a model he had never met in person until they boarded the plane. She was a true Texan, complete with curly locks of blonde hair, and an award-winning smile and personality. Meanwhile, Maurice was a piggish-appearing man with the personality to match. He had a slimy demeanor. His long nose gave way to speculation that he knew too much and wasn't afraid to tell for the right price. A true weasel.

"Minutes, Mr. Rove. Minutes that'll make themselves all the more warranted when we arrive."

Patrick Combs, the group's photographer, shrank into his chair. He didn't love flying but this was a gig he couldn't pass up. The money and exposure were both all too rewarding. He knew of Maurice Jackson's work and reputation. There was no doubt he would come back through customs as a man richer in wealth and power. He pulled out a cassette player from his bag and decided to listen to some tunes as he relaxed himself for the landing.

On the Type II tape, the song *Cruel Summer* by Bananarama played. It was fitting given the heat wave in Texas. July 1985 made for anything but a tranquil season.

Unbeknownst to him, right as he played the pop tune, the pilot came on over the intercom and announced that their flight would be delayed another ten minutes due to wind currents.

***

The Sun Chaser, boasted by a unique and polished design, drove through the warm waters of the Caribbean coast off of Coconut Cove. The peculiar rock formation with a mouth that made for the entrance to a cave always seemed to startle tourists. Those aboard the Sun Chaser knew better. There were tall tales surrounding the hot spot but that was as far as it went.

For a forty-two-foot fishing boat it could almost pass for a yacht. It had the same structure and appearance but the special modifications such as trolling rod holders, two on both the port and starboard, a bait box filled with raw fish and worms in another compartment within, and a table to fillet the catches. Below was pristine, almost like a mini multi-thousand-dollar hotel room. There was a bar, a viewing pane below the hull that showcased the natural beauty of underwater life, and cushioned seats wrapped around the entire deck.

It was not the ideal vessel for such activities and Hank Westin knew that. He chartered the boat not only to fishermen but parties as well. He knew the game and how to play it. There was a plentiful amount of cash coming in and it made any needed repairs more affordable in the long scheme of things.

Rusty, his Chinese mechanic, didn't care too much for the gigs, but he didn't complain. In fact, he barely made a noise at all beyond hoarse grunts. His expressions were how to tell what mood he was in.

"We've got to head back soon, fella!" Hank shouted from his spot in the console above.

"Aw, they're going to bite soon! I know it!" an overweight, balding, middle-aged man called back up to him.

"Mr. Mayor. I have an appointment arriving soon. I need to get back to the harbor A.S.A.P."

Mayor Brunswick was about to cast out again when Rusty walked over and snatched the pole out of his hand mid-swing.

"Hey, what gives? Give me back my pole, damnit!"

"Rusty!" Hank called to his only crew member worth his weight in salt. "Give the man back his pole."

He did not budge.

"Tell your monkey mechanic to relinquish my pole or I'll make it my personal mission to revoke any god damned license he has. If he has any at all," Brunswick sneered.

The man looked like he was about to lunge at the politician but was keeping himself in check. A mental war of disgust and disobedience was going on in his head no doubt. Then, without warning, he released his grip on the rod and returned it to its owner. He then gave a chipped-toothed grin and walked away.

"Neanderthal!" Brunswick cursed.

"Ah, Mayor. He was just messin' with ya," Hank said in a vain attempt to bring down the tension.

There was no response, just a man seething in his swivel chair.

Hank did not miss the opportune moment to start the engine and get out of there. He hoped the mayor was distracted with his own thoughts enough that he wouldn't notice the engine start up.

"Why do you even let him work for you?" Brunswick asked.

"Because he knows his way around a boat." Hank turned the keys slightly. "Better than any greenhorn or youthful individual I've seen around these parts."

Roaring to life, the engine puttered a bit but sounded good enough to take off.

"And what if I got rid of him?"

"Christ, Mayor. He was just teasing."

Brunswick turned and looked up at the captain. "I won't tolerate it." He then turned his attention to the sea. "The big one's out there. Cut that goddamned engine."

***

Water displacement disrupted the natural way of the current. The bobber lifted up and down out of the sea as the line that fed it outgrew slack. Holding the rod was a gentleman of culture but not class. He fit the old-style fisherman label down pat with a rustic appearance including blue jean overalls, a stained white shirt, and brown shoes that were caked in dirt and grime.

Captain Quinn kept his vessel, the Bow Dipper, afloat with pieces of half rotted wood and filthy fiberglass. He always feared his aptly named ship would live up to its title in due time. Somehow, he managed to keep it afloat. Some would say he held it together with tape and bubblegum, but others knew better. He was well-known for his precautions.

Never one to venture towards a risky situation, he avoided the likes of rocky coves, coral reefs, and even the shallow waters off the coastline.

Most knew though, that while he loved his hobbies, Quinn was a drug smuggler through and through. It was a trade he inherited from his older brother back in the early seventies. Therefore, the smelly old fisherman was maligned by his co-anglers for his actions and disliked throughout most of the community.

All but one person put up with his activities.

As he rolled a joint, he looked up and saw Hank Westin driving the Sun Chaser past the reefs. He also noticed that the mayor was aboard and quickly tucked the marijuana in a kettle pot below his feet, under the fighting chair.

He gave a half-hearted wave. The Sun Chaser passengers did not return the gesture.

When the boat was out of view, he fished out his joint and continued his pleasure cruise.

CHAPTER TWO

It fell to Earth with grace.

As the airplane dove down, the landing legs kicked out. Patrick could feel the wheels skidding on the runway. It was not the most extravagant aircraft, but it got them where they needed to be. Soon they were out of their seats and making their way towards the hatch which was open. The flight attendant spoke little English so when he introduced them to Mexico, the group just nodded in thanks.

Josh stretched his arms out wide, embracing the warm air. After his last photoshoot in Alaska and the chilly compartment of the plane they were unfortunately situated in, the heat was a welcome change. "Oh, you're lucky, Ginny. You probably would have become a popsicle in Alaska!"

She smiled. "Maybe. Thankfully you guys picked me up."

"Easy enough, sweetie. Your stop was sort of on the way, ya know?" Maurice chuckled.

Patrick, armed with his Nikon, immediately looked through the lens of his expensive handheld camera. It was like staring into a whole new world with a vignette encompassed around it. He snapped a few photographs of the fauna and some goats. As he did so, his feet kicked up sand. Only noticing when the camera began to cloud with the soot, he made an effort to walk like a normal human being.

"Quit dragging your feet, Pat!" Maurice called over to him. "We've got a schedule to keep."

A yellow cab with a sign that read *servicio de taxi* written in red against a white background pulled up to them. The taxi driver did not get out. Instead, he gestured from them to come over by snapping his head in a backwards tilt. It was an aggressive, impatient gesture. One that Maurice could not stand. He had to calm himself. This wasn't his homeland. Having grown up in California, he had only visited Mexico once and he did not like it then.

He was indifferent now.

The group approached the transportation vehicle with their luggage. Still the driver did not move. He just stared out the window, uncaring, unamused, the least bit hospitable. Patrick and Josh loaded the gear in the trunk while Ginny and Maurice piled in. The last bag was Ginny's, and it was excessively heavy.

"Christ, Ginny! What have you got in here?" Josh inquired as he heaved the travel case in.

"Just the essentials." She beamed and gave him a wink.

Josh thought Ginny was an alright looking woman. He was never a fan of the big hair that seemed to be sweeping the decade lately. Still, she had a dazzling smile and genuine personality. She was more Patrick's speed, but she was obviously way out of that man's league. Josh looked to him and chuckled.

"What's so funny?" Patrick asked as he placed his camera strap around his neck.

"Your mustache."

Patrick's eyes narrowed as he looked down. "What about it?"

"It doesn't even connect."

"Okay, mullet men!" Maurice shouted at the two from in the car. "Let's get moving!"

Both of them regarded their hair styles. They each had a mullet of varying degrees of length and shape. Josh had brown straight hair with a mullet that went down just below his neck while Patrick's was thick and curly with his black hair spiraling down towards his shoulders.

Josh finished loading the suitcase inside the taxi and then hopped in while Patrick scanned the area with his eyes. The airport really was a desolate area. His acid wash jeans were already getting dusty from the wind kicking up sand.

"C'mon. There are better sights to look at along the way." Ginny smiled at him, and his heart skipped a beat.

He quickly got in. The driver wasted no time in taking off. Patrick was still struggling with the buckle.

***

A cool afternoon gust blew above the surface. Nearby sailboats creaked and wavelets lightly tapped against jet skis. Ripples moved in a continuous formation, flowing in the direction of the wind. On shore, hair whipped around, and umbrellas tilted slightly. Some cursed under their breaths, others pondered if a hurricane was coming.

Beneath the shimmering surface, a massive figure, dark, monstrous, came in with the breeze. It stayed six hundred yards off the shoreline. As it perused back and forth, its ampullae of Lorenzini detected there were cables below. The electrical current garnered its attention enough to lower its body and change its directional path. As it closed in, its senses became overwhelmed. The current of electricity surged through the underwater cable like lightning through a tunnel.

Something else was there too. Though it could not decipher the inedible object, there was a familiar shape to it. Its eyes were never its strongest sensory organ. Vision was limited but, as its glassy black eyes began to examine the object, the more it became clear that it was recognizable.

There was no memory of it, just appearance.

Like chumming the same place more than once, fish become familiar. The bag was something it had consumed multiple times in the general area. A faint smell seeped out of the bag, one that garnered intrigue.

Parting its jaws slightly, the tiger shark consumed the bag of drugs. It then chomped down on the electrical cable and received a shock that snapped its body in an unnatural direction. Then, it charged away, quickly propelling itself forward and away from the cable with swift swaying of its caudal fin in short successions.

The electrical current stopped surging through the cable.

Hank Westin fixated on the hotel as he brought the boat in towards the harbor. It was one he always used as guidance to drive the boat in the direction of the shore. An old trick his grandfather taught him way back, it made for a fun way to impress tourists at the very least.

"Don't think I'll forget what transpired on this vessel of yours!" Mayor Brunswick shouted over the increasingly booming noise of the engine.

Neither Hank nor Rusty paid him any mind.

Suddenly, the boat shifted in an unexpected direction.

"Hey, what gives?" Brunswick screamed. "I thought you had a good reputation for driving your boat, Westin?"

"There's something below us," Hank explained.

He then eased on the throttle as Rusty came out from the cabin below. The two men looked at each other and nodded. The mayor noticed.

"What gives? What was it?"

"An old friend," Hank said.

Shivers ran down Brunswick's spine. He was visibly shaken by the remark. "Which old friend is that?"

"I don't know," Hank said. "Many a fish holds a grudge in this general area. They don't like me."

They don't like your bait, Rusty thought.

Soon, Hank started the boat up again. Eventually, they made their way into the bay and were closing in on one of the docks. They passed a jetty where a bum was sitting on the edge. He was seemingly contemplating his life. Rusty looked to Brunswick who paid neither him nor the homeless man any mind.

A lot of good he's doing for this country. He isn't even a native, Rusty lamented. The mayor was indeed born in Mexico. His birth certificate even said so, not that most bought into it. He won by a hair and, as far as he was concerned, it was too close. Something was not right about the election. He just wished he had the voice to speak his concerns.

"Rusty, grab the rope. We're nearing the slick now," Hank called down to him.

The man was lost in his own thoughts, so much so that he hadn't realized how close they were. He grabbed the rope and tossed it onto the piling with such swift accuracy that Brunswick did not have time to fully get off the fighting chair. When he did, the handyman was already pulling them closer towards the dock.

"Fast little guy," he admitted.

You should see how fast I can knock your lights out, Rusty smirked to himself.

Brunswick took it as a sign of common humor and patted him on the back. "You and I will get along just fine."

It took every fiber of Rusty's being not to spin around and live up to his thoughts.

Hank descended the ladder just as a taxi pulled into the parking lot on shore. "Perfect! We're right on time!"

The mayor offloaded with the speed of a slug and the appearance to boot. Rusty begrudgingly helped him over the port side so he wouldn't slip off and tumble into the water. For being a man of undesirable height, he had the girth of a hippopotamus.

As Brunswick shambled his way onto land, the harbor master greeted him and helped him to his limousine where his chauffeur stood, door open and smile ready. The mayor shoved his tackle box and rod into the driver's hands. "Let's get back, Todd. I don't want to be late for the meeting."

Wasting no time, Todd shut the door and hopped in the car. He then drove off as soon as the group of four climbed out of the taxi. Their stride to step onto the dock was long but not uncomfortably so.

"I'm surprised that fat ass got on here so easily!" Josh laughed.

"That *fat ass* is our infamous mayor of Leyenda Island, Eddie Brunswick." Hank approached them.

"But he isn't Mexican," Patrick brought up.

"You don't have to be Mexican to be in politics here. Like America, you can be Mestizo without being of Mexican blood. As long as you were born here, you qualify," Hank explained.

"Interesting," Ginny said with genuine interest.

Hank took one look at her and was already second guessing the tour. "I have two big rules on my boat. Numero uno is there can be no illegal drugs. Weed, cocaine, none of that fun stuff." He gave a half-hearted smile. "Booze is okay, though. Second, this is not a playhouse. No porn."

Maurice returned the smile. "No worries, Mr. Westin. We're here for a professional modeling shoot. Nothing more."

With a quick handshake sealing the deal, Hank helped them with their luggage. Patrick stared out off the side of the dock as they made their way out further and further. As they did, the water became noticeably darker. It was somewhat eerie.

"This isn't the Bahamas," Hank stated. "The water is clearer the further you go. Right here, there's a long dark patch of vegetation. Seaweed and such. Once we're a few miles out, you'll be able to see the bottom from the boat."

"Is there no vegetation in the deeper water?" Ginny asked.

"Oh, there is. It's mostly around the coral reefs though. Which reminds me." Hank stopped and turned to Maurice. "You're paying double for this trip, correct?"

"Yes."

"Good, I don't want my windows smashing against the rocks. If I acquire damage on this trip, it'll cost you, but it'll mostly cost me. So, no asking for changing directions. I know the area well and will bring you to the best spots. Not at the expense of my boat or your safety though."

"I appreciate your knowledge, Mr. Westin. I do believe this will be a worthwhile trip."

When they approached the Sun Chaser, Maurice clapped his hands together. "Beautiful! This is perfect! I was going for a modern yet somewhat rustic look!"

"Then you'll get the best of both worlds aboard my boat!" Hank stated proudly.

Rusty came out of the cabin and waved.

"Who's this cheerful fellow?" Maurice asked.

"His name is Ju-Han, but I just refer to him as Rusty. He seems to appreciate it more. He's my handyman and friend. Anything you need fixed, he can do so. Don't ask him to say much. He can't speak."

"English?" Josh asked.

"Not English, not Spanish. Not at all, period. His throat was cut when he was eleven."

"How do you know that if he can speak English or Spanish or not then?" Josh inquired.

Ginny was about to object and apologize for his rude behavior, giving him a glare. Hank noticed and held his hand up in a peaceful gesture. "It's alright. I know he's mute because I impaired him."

The group just stared.

"Me and him were out fishing and he, well, he stepped on a puffer fish. He fell in the water, and it swam to him and got embedded in his throat. I had to cut it out and sew him back up. He barely survived. We shortly moved out here after his father disowned him. He thought he was useless if he couldn't speak."

"That's horrible," Ginny said.

"The 1960s was a different time in Japan. I was a foreign exchange student, and he was my only friend. We were just about to graduate high school, so it was high time we left anyway."

They stood in silence.

"No need to dwell on the past. Let's look forward to the future!" Hank said cheerfully. "All aboard the Sun Chaser!"

CHAPTER THREE

The stuffiness irritated her.

Rosa Alvarez sat in the office of questionable temperature wishing she were anywhere but. On her desk was a picture of her parents, siblings, and close family at a cookout from a few years ago. It was a celebratory day for she had just been made lieutenant detective. Her position was stationed in New Mexico, closer to home.

As she looked around her desk, she saw the plaque with her name followed by her title engraved on it. It had an embossed shine overall. It was a beautiful piece she continuously cleaned along with her drawers, desktop, and random items around her. It was the cleanest spot in the whole station.

There was a knock on her open door suddenly and she jolted up a bit.

"Sorry, I didn't mean to scare you, Lieutenant Alvarez." Her partner and friend, Santos Barca, stood at the doorway.

At five-foot-two, he was barely an intimidating presence. It was what was underneath that scared people. His short temper along with violent outbursts truly made him a force to be feared. He would've been let off the force a long time ago had it not been for Rosa.

"What's up, small boat?" She gave a slight smirk.

"When are you going to stop poking fun at my last name?"

"I'll do so when you start calling me *Lieutenant* Alvarez," Rosa stated.

"Dream on." Santos chuckled and took a seat on the other side of her desk.

"Did you need something?"

Her partner grinned from ear to ear. "We've got a lead."

Rosa stared at him impatiently. "Who?"

"A random caller by the name of Burt. The man said he saw someone diving off his property."

"That's not too unusual," she said.

"Yeah, you're right." Santos stood up and began to make his way out of the room. He stopped and placed his hand on the doorframe. "I mean, I don't think it means anything that they were diving at night near an underwater power cable."

Her interest visibly piqued. "Don't be a wise ass, what else happened?"

Santos smiled. "The caller was a nut. He said he had cameras set up all around his beach condo. Waste of money if you ask me. Anyway, when night comes, his cameras adjust to the change in light."

"Night vision!" Rosa beamed.

"Very good, Detective," he said sarcastically.

"Did he get the perpetrator on camera or not?"

"Our guys got the camera footage and, lo and behold, there it was."

"It..." she inquired.

"The bag of drugs."

"Who was on the boat?"

"The man holding said bag was decked out in black fatigue and the footage was blurry as all hell. Again, our boys are going over the footage. Trying to zoom in and clean it up."

"Any idea what kind of drugs were in the bag?"

"It was a duffle bag. No idea."

"Damnit, Santos. For all we know it could've been personal belongings the culprit didn't want anymore." She placed her pointer fingers on her temple and gave them a hard rub.

"There's more."

"A slip up?" Rosa looked at him.

"Perhaps. We aren't sure yet, but it looked like the guy was using a radio. Maybe to confirm the job was completed?" he suggested.

Rosa got up and pulled open her filing cabinet. She flipped through the folders until she reached behind them. In one slow movement, she pulled out a card.

"What's that?" Santos asked.

"Remember when I hooked up with that gun shop owner for a week and a half?"

He laughed. "That redneck had more guns than brain cells."

"Anyway," Rosa's voice trailed. "He is also a licensed pilot. We could hire him as a surveyor off the coast. Maybe he'll scare them off."

"Alvarez, honey, I know you and I go way back. Believe me when I tell you, that is one of the dumbest excuses I've heard to see a guy again."

"Damnit, I think he can help!"

"Give him a jingle then. I'm dying to see how this plays out," Santos chuckled.

"I will." Rosa glared at him as she reached for her phone.

***

Hank brought the Sun Chaser to a stop. As the boat slowed, Ginny peered over the side. "It's so clear!"

"Just like the captain said!" Patrick smiled.

Josh, too, was taken aback by the sheer vastness of the underwater world. It teemed with life and natural perfection. He looked further out and noticed he could make out a formation in the water. "What's that?"

"Something we're not getting any closer to," Hank began. "It's a coral reef, one that has an arch. It's a perfect half circle in the ground. The rocks have plenty of embedded shells and plant life surrounding it. It'd make for great pictures."

"I wish we brought scuba suits now," Ginny sighed.

"Not in the budget," Maurice said, looking down at his paper pad.

It was listed with all the shots needed for the day. They were accounted for by time and weather. Some shots were to feature the sun glowing behind Ginny, others were moodier with Josh sitting on the gunwale, the moon behind him. Maurice had it all planned in his head. All he had to do was direct and have Patrick take the pictures.

"Is this a good spot?" Hank asked.

"It's perfect!" Maurice beamed with excitement.

Rusty watched as Ginny tore off her shirt and jean short shorts. She wore a red, white and blue halter bikini top with matching bottoms. Her tanned body was alluring. He fought to control himself and his nether regions. All the while, Patrick fought to not look at her, trying to be polite, but it was becoming increasingly harder as she bent over to dig through her purse. Instead of pressing his luck, he looked down at his camera and adjusted the settings to help it adapt to the harsh sunlight.

"What're you doin' there?" Hank asked.

"Oh, um, I'm turning down the brightness, so the photographs aren't over exposed."

"Back in my day, they had cameras like that. They weighed a good thirty, forty pounds though."

"Some still do," Patrick chuckled.

Maurice clapped his hands together. "We almost ready, everyone?"

"We're all good." Josh finished pulling off his shirt to reveal his oily abs.

Patrick nodded. "Just making a couple of last-minute adjustments."

"Well, hurry up. Time's a tickin', sun's a settin'."

"It's only eleven o' clock," Patrick argued.

"Yeah, and we could be out here all day. Chop chop!"

***

Loco listened to the crazed customer as he explained, for the umpteenth time, how his scope broke. There was no end to how he screamed that he wanted his demands met. He was desperately trying not to roll his eyes.

Arnold finally came out of the office. The customer seemed relieved.

"Tell your buddy here that either I get a refund or I don't come back, Arnold," he ordered.

"First off, you don't come in here barking orders. Second, and most importantly, don't yell at my *buddy*."

"Arnie, what the fuck?"

"Don't cuss in my store, third strike and you're out, *buddy*!"

The customer was taken aback.

"Do I need to get the police involved?"

He backed off, making his way quickly out the door.

"No cussing allowed?" Loco tilted his head, confused.

"I don't give a shit." Arnold patted him on the shoulder. "You handled that well."

Arnold chuckled and got back to his work. Just then, the phone next to him rang and he jumped. He picked it up in one swift motion, making it seem he was angry. He was the complete opposite, instead happy for any kind of potential customer. Business had hit a slow patch when the new shopping plaza opened nearby. In it, its very own gun shop.

"Crazy Caliber, this is Arnie. How can I help you?"

"You're going by Arnie now?" a familiar female voice was heard on the other end.

"Rosa?" His heart skipped a beat.

"The one and only."

There was a pause.

"What can I do for you, Detective?" he said in an all-business tone with a hint of flirtation.

"I'm a lieutenant detective now, Ray."

"Even better!" He beamed. "So, how can I be of service. . . Lieutenant?"

"We need an aerial survey for a few nights."

Arnold thought about it. The chance to meet up with the sexy Latina again made his heart ache. He hadn't had a love-making companion for a while. He turned to Loco who looked apprehensive to ask who was on the other line.

"You do realize it's almost the Fourth of July."

"What has that got to do with anything?"

"Well, if it's additional security you're looking for then you're barking up the wrong tree. I specialize in legit crime searching. Murder, rape."

"Drugs." Her voice trailed off.

"Oh no. Don't tell me you're chasing *him* again."

"Well, someone's got to."

There was only a second to think it over when Rosa spoke again. *"I have witness testimony to the drug dumping."*

"Is the witness credible?"

"They're local."

"That doesn't mean anything."

"Look, I know it's a long shot, but I have to get this done. Can you help me or not?"

He could tell how personal this was for her. Her voice had risen an octave and her breath had become short. "I'll come down there, but I want you to go over with me, by map, exactly where I'm scouting."

"It's right off the shoreline near some underwater power cables."

"Still need more detail. I can be there by tomorrow morning."

"Okay," she agreed.

"I hope there's compensation for this gig."

"Of course."

"Good, because I'm closing down shop to come down there."

"I thought your buddy would've been able to hold down the store?"

There's that word again. . . buddy, Arnold thought.

"He's not watching the gun store alone. No, we're closing shop and he'll come with me."

There was an underlining annoyance when she sighed. *"Please hurry. I want to catch them before they change locations."*

"See you tomorrow morning."

She said her goodbyes and hung up. Arnold took a few seconds before pulling the phone away from his ear and then placing it back on its cradle. He turned to Loco.

"Road trip?"

"Pack your bathing suit. We leave tonight."

***

With the turn of a knob, the volume on the radio rose. Def Leppard's *Photograph* started with a low hanging guitar strum followed by slow drum banging. The song built up as Ginny danced, parading around in her American flag bikini. Josh watched her while he sat on the gunwale. He was aroused mentally and physically and wanted to take her into the cabin below. He knew how to control his feelings when it came to that sort of emotional, impulsive reaction though.

Patrick had no choice but to stare at her through the camera. The lens showed her elegant motion as she swayed her hips and began to perform a belly dance. She got close to the camera and even placed a hand on his shirt collar to pull him closer. She pursed her lips and, at first, he thought she was going to kiss him. Instead, she kissed in front of the camera. He felt piggish. The whole shoot was trashy, and Maurice knew he did not like that sort of gig.

"Don't be a prude," Maurice called out to him. "Get in there."

Face flushed with embarrassment, he walked closer to Ginny. She smiled seductively; it was almost friendly, welcoming. He zoomed in on her beautiful face as she mouthed the words *later*. His heart skipped a beat, and he almost dropped the camera.

"What're you doing, Combs? Hold your damn equipment!" Maurice yelled.

His camera fell to his side, facing out towards sea. He did not see what the camera saw. A twenty-inch fin. "I need a minute."

Josh laughed. "So much for me thinking you were gay."

The remark invigorated as well as enraged Patrick. He lifted the camera back up and continued filming. This time, he found his hips were swaying to the tune.

Up near the console, Hank chuckled. "I'm getting too old for this shit."

Rusty smirked.

"Very funny, I know. Say, why don't you grab them a few more beers from the cooler below."

The mechanic scowled. He begrudgingly climbed down the ladder and into the cabin. Maneuvering around the viewing window on the floor, he reached the cooler. That's when something caught his eye. The light had returned underwater. It was as if something had been blocking it when he came down, a huge shadow. It would have had to have been something massive to block out all that natural brightness. His blood ran cold, and he quickly came out of the cabin.

"What's up with you, man?" Josh asked as the mechanic nearly ran into him.

"Rusty, where are the beers?" Hank then noticed the fear on his face. "What is it?"

He made no inkling of trying to gesture what happened down there. Instead, he walked below and came back up with an armful of beers. One for each of the four on the deck and one for himself.

CHAPTER FOUR

The murk below.

Under the noses of the politicians, the lower class suffered. The random fundraisers to help them were a successful attempt to line their pockets further. They had deep pockets to fill. Ollie Morgan knew this, as did her brother, Eddie Brunswick. Lewis Morgan, her devoted husband, was left in the dark somewhat. He had a fraction of an idea but didn't trust his gut impulse. He was a peace activist back in the day. The things Ollie had done and still did would be enough to make him want her dead.

As he drove on his way home from work, he noticed a homeless man. He was sitting on the end of a dock, staring down at the muddy shoreline. For unknown reasons, Lewis drove over into the parking lot and sat there. The man didn't seem to mind. He had a sadness that covered his very being. Lewis wondered what drove a man to such depression. He was told the community they had was successful and thriving.

He then thought that perhaps he had family issues. Part of him wanted to get out and talk to the man. This impulse was quickly tucked away when he saw the bum reach into his pocket and produce a revolver. Lewis covered his mouth in shock at what happened next.

Bang.

The right side of the man's head blew away in chunks of flesh and brain matter. He then tumbled forward and fell off the dock, into the sea.

Lewis quickly got out and ran out towards the spot. When he looked over to the side, what he saw made him freeze in fear. A massive head with a mouth filled with rows and rows of teeth snatched the man and darted away. The speed mixed with the size of the fish caused a spray of seawater that splashed Lewis. He fell on his rear and nearly slipped off the side himself. He managed to get to his feet and run back to his car.

For several minutes he contemplated what to do. He figured he should call the police but realized Ollie would not have liked that. He, instead, drove home. He passed several pay phones along the way, several opportunities.

The predator was not content with its morsel. As it pressed onward, the goliath gargantuan picked up some rather strange vibrations. The source was not from heartbeats or splashing. It was a rhythmic booming, a beat.

Piquing the shark's interest, it changed direction. The very act of doing so caused a swell of water to spin as it moved in a circular motion – an underwater tornado. When the shark completed its turn, its tail swung outward, straightening the fish out. Then, as the body motioned and the caudal fin swayed, the water displacement returned to normal.

"I got it to work, honey!" the woman shouted to her husband from the sea.

He gave her the thumbs up and watched as her belly bulge bounced in the surf. He figured it was not good for the baby but was no expert. Her doctor had recommended music and the ocean, and she combined the two. A wacky idea but it did not seem to be causing her any discomfort.

The keyboards shrieked in a brash, yet pleasant harmony followed by the single slam of a drum repeatedly boomed as *Separate Ways* by Journey began.

Marie Cortez bounced up and down as she cheered at the start of the vocals. She was a Steve Perry enthusiast.

Her husband, Lee, didn't see the appeal but didn't mind some of the tunes such as the one his wife was currently jamming out to.

"Be careful of our child, Marie!"

"He's fine!"

You're eight months pregnant though, he thought but kept it to himself.

She began to raise her hands and began to move them with the radio, side to side.

"Be careful! Don't get it wet!" Lee called out to her.

Thankful for the wavelets that brushed past her and against the shoreline, Lee found himself relieved that the chop was not too bad and that his wife was enjoying herself.

Then the chorus came, and she began to hop up and down onto the seabed. She was creating more waves than the ocean itself, but she did not worry over it.

He looked around the remote beach and saw only one other couple and a child, presumably theirs. They had long hair, so it was hard to tell if they were a boy or girl. He admired how they all seemed to be in perfect harmony. He could not wait for that.

A splashing sound caught everyone's attention. Lee turned to his wife to see her looking out at the sea. Small fish-looking creatures were swimming around.

Lee wished he had his camera.

Marie was enchanted at first. She assumed they were a sign of good fortune and luck. Something seemed off though, as if they were alert.

On the shore, Lee noticed this too. "Marie, maybe it's time to come back in, huh?"

"They are just dolphins, babe. I can't tell what they're trying to do though," Marie called back to him.

The dolphins then began to be erratic, splashing and carefully nudging against her. The radio got soaked in the process just as the song reached the climax.

"Darn it." She lowered the radio to examine it.

"Marie, forget the damn thing. I think they want you out of the water." He referred to the dolphins.

Then, out of nowhere, the dolphins scattered. Marie did not notice.

"I think it's brok…"

She was lifted out of the water. Not by a dolphin but a massive shark. The needle-like teeth pierced her skin and blood poured out instantly. The colossal fish had charged with such speed that it had pushed her towards shore nearly ten yards.

Lee wasted no time and screamed after her, making his way into the sea. He trudged through the water.

The shark remained above the surf with her in its mouth. It was like it was teasing Lee to come get his wife. It hadn't bitten down yet. Its prey just lay limp in its mouth, clearly in shock.

"Marie! I'm coming, honey."

Suddenly, the great fish pushed itself out of the water even closer towards Lee and the shore. Soon, it was practically directly over him.

Then came the chomp.

It was a slow, slicing motion that came down on Marie like a compressor or a jack inching closer and closer to losing its hold on a car. A wall of blood sprayed all over Lee as teeth pierced her big belly. Gelatinous looking flesh and bodily fluids spilled out of her as the shark completed its bite. Then, it was as if it were never there. The shark was gone, as was Marie and her and Lee's child. It had slipped under the surface with a grace most would find hauntingly beautiful. Lee could only see red before he passed out.

A few hours had passed before he came back around. He was surrounded by unfamiliar faces and lights. After a minute he put two and two together and realized he was in a hospital. A nurse was looking into his eyes with her humble penlight, bringing it back and forth. There were signs of distress as his eyes rapidly shot back and forth. It was not confusion; he was reliving the memory of what had just happened to him.

"Where's Marie?" Lee asked, his voice slightly above a whisper.

A doctor came over and looked at him with saddened eyes. They seemed genuine. "I'm sorry, Mr. Cortez."

"Did they find it?"

"You mean them?" the doctor corrected him.

"It was only one animal that killed my wife."

"The report from the family that brought you here said they saw your wife was killed by blunt force trauma caused by a pod dolphins."

Despite the grim circumstances, Lee couldn't help but laugh, rather scoff at the doctor. "It was a shark. A fucking big, cruel shark."

He began to sit upright but the nurse sat him back with her hand lightly pressing on his chest.

"It was the biggest fish I have ever seen in my life."

"Mr. Cortez, please be rational. The family said your wife was only fifty yards out at most."

"So?"

"A shark of the size you're describing would not travel so close to shore to eat a human being."

Lee began to ponder on it. "What about all the blood?"

"The family said you were covered in barnacles and blood. They saw you passed out in the ocean where your wife was."

"How could dolphins cause damage enough to make my wife bleed the way she did?"

"I'll admit, it is odd," the doctor admitted. "Apparently, they found several dolphins dead not too far away. They were infected with something. It's being investigated now by police."

"Oh my god," Lee groaned as he lay on his side.

The doctor motioned for the nurse to let him be. They both walked out, shutting the lights off as they left.

***

Easi Ortega watched as the massive fan on the wall near the ceiling spun. It welcomed a breeze that, no matter how minuscule, cooled him down. July was already starting to outdo last month's record-breaking heat. As he stared at the circular rotation of the blades, the door to the warehouse busted open. Two of his men, Rafael, and Philipe, dragged a barely conscious man across the cement floor. His bare feet rubbed against it. Scabs ripped as he created a blood trail.

Both henchmen approached and tossed the barely lucid man onto the floor. He struggled to his knees.

Easi looked at him without pity.

"You fucked up. Big time."

"The packages weren't supposed to leak."

"I'm not as worried about that as I am about the fact that you were spotted by a local who reported your suspicious activity to the police."

At Easi's side was a beautiful woman. One of elegance. She had a darkness behind her eyes that no man trusted. She was loyal to Easi though and that was all he cared about. She reached behind his chair and withdrew a pistol with a silencer attached.

"Sofia, no." The cowering man quivered with fear.

She casually walked around his desk. "That's Ms. Beltran to you, you pathetic waste of talent."

"I'm sorry, Ms. Beltran. Please, have mercy. I can fix this."

"Wait." Easi held up a hand. "I want to hear his ingenious plan to fix what he messed up."

The man sat silent.

"We're waiting," Sofia said impatiently.

He took a breath and realized he had no idea how to fix his mistake. "I'll see you in hell."

"Nice try," Easi continued. "If I wanted you dead, your blood would be splattered on the floor along with your brains and ball fluid. No, I'm going to have to teach you a lesson before we can continue this charade you call a partnership." He then nodded to Sofia who quickly aimed and shot his pleading left hand.

He let out a howling cry.

"You're going down to retrieve the product. They cannot be discovered by the police."

"The drugs are too hot to be moved right now. With it leaking, anyone who goes down there will be affected by its contents."

"So, you'll come up with something, ya?" Easi chuckled. "If you accomplish this, you can consider our contract void and your freedom in its place."

"I'll need an escort."

"You'll get none. I'll provide you with the gun that blew your fingers off but that's it."

"Poetic," Rafael chimed in with a giggle.

"Screw you. I'll be dead either way."

"Mr. Quinn, if you weren't so invaluable at the moment, I'd end your life for your lurid remark," Easi said and then nodded to his henchmen who picked him up off the ground and brought him back outside.

CHAPTER FIVE

Something was amiss.

As Hank sat there, chipping away at a small piece of wood, carving out a shiv, he couldn't help but stare at Rusty from time to time. He was leaning against the ladder to the upper deck. His usual spot was on the gunwale or cabin below. It appeared as though he was fearful of the surrounding sea. It was uncharacteristic of the man. Beyond that, it made the paying passengers feel on edge. They were still enjoying themselves though the grim looks from Rusty did not bode well for entertainment.

Snap.

The stick broke, the small blade sliced upward and cut Hank's thumb. "Ah shit." He quickly waved his hand in the air.

When he returned his attention to the deck below, he saw Rusty and the passengers staring at him. "That's nothing!" He held up his hand. "You should've seen ol' Pete getting his hand caught in a net of hooks."

Rusty's eyes rolled to the side.

"Who's ol' Pete?" Patrick inquired.

"He was an old fisherman that used illegal methods to catch more than his fill."

"Was?" Ginny asked.

"Yeah, he eventually retired and became a representative for a corporation. There was just one thing he didn't like about it."

"What's that?" Patrick asked.

"Their slogan was hook 'em," Hank chuckled.

Patrick, Ginny, and even Josh laughed. Maurice just stood there, stoic.

"Dad jokes later please. We need to get back to work," he said.

"It's alright, Maurice. I have to get the camera out anyway. It'll take me a few minutes to get her set up," Patrick explained.

"Make it quick," Maurice said.

"Yes, sir." He saluted him and then headed into the cabin below.

Josh grabbed his radio and fast forwarded a few tunes to find a new song on his mix tape to play. He was torn between a few of them, so he decided to select at random. *Somebody's Watching Me* by Rockwell came on. The spooky tune had an interesting beat, and the vocals were mostly talking but it was enough to act as filler until Patrick came back.

Patrick took out his bag and sorted through its contents. The radio next to him was barely audible as it reported the local news. He didn't pay it too much mind.

Breaking news: a woman, age twenty-three, eight-months pregnant, was killed off Juana Beach. Reports say that a pod of dolphins surrounded the woman and fatally attacked her. Police say to be on the look out for at least four dolphins acting strange.

He stood silent, holding his camera in hand. The thought of a woman being killed by a creature that was normally friendly was sad enough but to have the living person inside her be taken as well as heartbreaking. He knew he had to warn Hank and Rusty but the nagging feeling that Maurice would take the idea of heading back as mutiny at the very least pulled at him. He would most likely throw a fit and demand to stay.

Putting aside his boss' opinion on the matter, he decided he had to do the right thing. He began towards the cabin doorway when he heard the engine roar to life and Maurice barking orders. He quickened his pace and ran into Ginny who was sniffling.

"It's awful!"

"You heard? About the pregnant woman, I mean?" Patrick asked her.

"What pregnant woman? There's a dolphin out there caught in a net," Ginny explained.

The two walked out onto the deck and stood, looking out the starboard side. Hank and Rusty were hanging off the side, their waists pressed against the gunwale for support. Patrick rushed up to them. "Get away from it!"

"What're you talking about, boy? It's a dolphin," Hank scoffed.

"They just said on the local news that a pod of dolphins just killed a pregnant woman and that something seemed wrong with them."

Hank and Rusty shared a glance. The two then looked at the dolphin. It seemed distressed but not crazed. It wasn't until they looked into its eyes that something seemed off. "Its eyes are red," Hank stated.

"How can you tell? Aren't their eyes black? Like entirely dark?" Josh asked.

"It doesn't matter! Just cut the thing loose so we can go to the next spot," Maurice ordered.

"Its eyes are severely reddened. It's like they're inflamed," Hank explained.

Patrick turned to Maurice. "What new location?"

Maurice chuckled. "It's a surprise."

Rusty reached forward, his trusty utility knife in hand. He began to cut away at the netting as the dolphin glared at him. It seemed to know that he was helping but that it was for its own self gain.

Splash.

Everyone but Rusty looked to the port side where some water spray splashed upward. Three small fins began to make their way around the vessel. Patrick reached for Rusty's belt and yanked him backwards. The two fell back on each other. All the while, the dolphin that was in the net dove down and managed to free itself, untangling the net as it slid off its slippery skin. The four dolphins then regrouped and darted out to sea.

"That was too close!" Hank shouted.

"Just take us to the next location. They won't follow us," Maurice explained.

"Don't whales hold grudges or something? I saw it in a movie a few years back," Josh stated.

"That was an orca, but the same principles apply," Hank said.

"Why are they holding a grudge? We didn't do anything to them!" Ginny wondered, her voice trembling.

"Maybe not." Hank looked out at the water. "But something ain't right about them and I don't trust it. We're heading back."

"The hell we are!" Maurice yelled. "We didn't come all this way for a measly few hours."

"I'll add a day free of charge," Hank offered.

"I have to be back to California to present the pictures to my producers by Wednesday," Maurice said. "It's already the Saturday before. I don't have an extra day."

"Can we please add a couple of hours tomorrow, Marty," Ginny suggested.

"To take pictures in the dark? Are you blonde and dumb? No. We already have the next two days as all day charters. This isn't going to happen. We're staying out here and that's final." Maurice was screaming at this point.

The group sat in silence momentarily.

"If you don't, we'll take our business elsewhere," Maurice sneered.

Rusty knew they needed the money and shot Hank a glare. The captain did not look back. Instead, he turned and made his way over to Rusty and Patrick, helping both of them up. "You're insane if you want to stick around but it's your choice."

"You got that right," Maurice chuckled.

"And now for something a bit more pleasant. Here's Motörhead with their catchy 1979 hit Overkill," the personality over the radio said as Phil Taylor's inspirational drumming began to drive the song forward. The guitars and bass then kicked in and Lemmy's voice rocketed on with his signature, guttural tone.

"That's more pleasant?" Patrick said.

Ginny giggled. "Depends on one's taste, I guess."

The two shared a smile.

***

Ollie Morgan sat on a fold out chair on the patio. Overlooking Castaway Bay, the patio was as old as the mansion itself. A structure built of old brick, the interior had been updated over the years. It adapted along with the owners over time.

As she absorbed the sun by using a sheet of tinfoil, she felt content. It was a rare feeling to have lately with all the discussion of border control and racism against her for not being of native blood. The shipment of illegal drugs across to her island was a more pressing matter to her though.

It wasn't that she wanted them gone though.

The sound of a door shutting on the first floor grabbed her attention but for only a second. It was about time for her husband to come home and, she expected, a quiet evening to follow. Usually, he would make his way to the fridge, pull out a beer, and sit on the couch, kicking off his shoes and turning on his favorite program, *Murder She Wrote*. Tonight was different. He walked out onto the patio and stared out at the bay.

She looked up at him and forced a smile. "Hello, sweetie. How was your day?"

"We need to talk," he said coldly.

"Oh?"

Lewis walked over to the bar hut with two unlit tiki torches in either side and, with trembling hands, poured himself a brandy. "I saw a man kill himself today."

"That's awful." She feigned shock.

"Don't lie, it's one less mentally disturbed individual the island would have to deal with. For you, that means a percentage ends up in your pocket."

"Don't patronize me!" Ollie shouted suddenly.

"I'm not trying to but you make it so easy."

"What has gotten into you?"

"It wasn't just the man blowing his fucking brains out that worried me. It's what happened after."

"Did he get robbed, raped? What's so bad that could've happened to him after he was already dead?"

"Eaten."

"I beg your pardon."

"A shark. A big fucking shark ate him."

Ollie turned to him for the first time. She hadn't bothered even looking in his direction before, let alone indulging in his story. "How big are we talking?"

"I'm no shark expert, but it was, well, as big as a bus."

"A shark the size of a bus, with teeth and an appetite for the mentally unstable islanders is swimming off these waters?" she chuckled.

"Yes! You'd better believe it too. You should've seen it; it grabbed him and dragged him away with minimal effort. I can't imagine what kind of damage a shark like that could cause if it came closer to a populated area."

She just looked at him.

"Ollie, believe me. The thing is a threat to the entire island."

"Where did this happen?" A man's voice asked from the sliding doors.

Both turned to see Eddie Brunswick standing in the doorway.

"Don't worry, big brother. It's not real," Ollie said.

"Bullshit! Ed, the thing is a monster!" Lewis stated.

"Why did it eat him? I mean, I haven't heard of a shark attack around here for around ten, maybe even eleven years," Eddie tried to reason with him.

"Maybe it's sick? A shark that big isn't normal," Lewis suggested.

"I don't know." Eddie took a seat near his sister. "A bus with teeth, huh?"

"Doesn't matter. We've got bigger fish to fry." Ollie looked back out at the bay, her shades covering her icy blue eyes that matched her soul.

"Oh yeah?" Eddie turned to her slightly, interest piqued.

"Two words: Dolphin attack."

"Dolphins? What the hell is going on on this island?" Eddie wondered.

"I am not sure, but I do know this. If a pod of dolphins is attacking people, then they are a deadlier threat than a scavenging great white."

"Tiger," Lewis said softly.

"I beg your pardon?" Eddie inquired.

"It had stripes. It was a tiger shark."

CHAPTER SIX

It graced the skies.

Arnold Ray piloted with ease. The AS350 utility helicopter was flown through the airspace after being cleared by the Mexican airline control tower. It was only after giving up their guns to be sent through customs that they were allowed to do so. As far as Arnold was concerned, Rosa had some explaining to do. He thought she had connections where it counted. Apparently, there were things that went beyond even her control on the island of Leyenda.

Sand particles kicked up as he brought the chopper around the landing platform. The yellow markings were on the police station's own backlot behind a shooting range and in front of an old storage shed. The area beyond the range was barely used anymore. Too much tension going on within the town, let alone the country and its neighbors.

As Loco stared down at the dirt ground below, he wondered who exactly she had informed of their arrival. Some of the officers seemed on guard but others were content. It was a mix of worry and expectations, almost as if they did not know they were coming.

The helicopter's skids touched down and a few officers approached quickly, ducking their heads to avoid the spinning rotor blades. Rosa approached just as Arnold stepped out of the pilot's side door.

Police men and women unloaded the aircraft as Loco helped. Rosa and Arnold slowly closed the distance between each other. Arnold was having a hard time averting his gaze to be casual.

"Wanna take a picture? It'll last longer," she chuckled.

"I missed you too," Arnold smirked.

"That's all well and good," Loco approached with a duffle bag of clothing, "but what about our guns?"

"We're basically an island that's not too far from shore. Someone's got to be in charge," she continued. "They will be in customs for a couple more days at the most."

Loco grumbled as he walked back to the helicopter to unload more gear.

Arnold took his aviators off. "You're looking good, Lieutenant."

"As are you, Arnie."

He smiled.

"Listen, can we break up the chitchat and make with the hotel? I'm sore from sitting in that crammed cockpit," Loco called out to them.

"For sure!" Rosa told him and then turned to make her way back to her police cruiser.

"Shotgun!" Arnie exclaimed.

As they approached, Arnie opened the front passenger seat and saw another familiar face. Deputy Santos Barca sat there with a grin. "I don't think so, my friend."

"Hey, small boat. Long time no see," Arnie stated.

Santos rolled his eyes and then got out and opened the back of the vehicle for them.

As they made their way out of the heliport, Rosa couldn't help but look at Arnold in her rear-view mirror. He had aged an insignificant amount, still appearing ten years younger than he actually was. His big arms and muscular build could almost rival the movie titans of the current decade. Though there was a longing in his eyes, she would fight her impulses. She had convinced herself that their relationship was a one-time fling that just so happened to last for a week and a half. Only a small part of her wanted to try it out again. There was no denying the flirtatious exuberance that he presented. She may have even pushed it herself. She carefully reeled back to make the car ride less awkward.

"How's business going?" she asked.

"It's goin'," Arnold began. "We have our profitable days and loyal customers like most businesses in the area."

"That's nice." Rosa smiled.

"Gun shop? Am I right?" Santos asked.

"Yes, we own one of the biggest stores in the mall."

"In size or profit margin?"

"Erm, I…" Arnold began.

"Why do you have to be so nosey, Deputy?" Rosa intervened.

"Sorry, second nature I guess," he chuckled.

For the next five minutes, the car was silent, exactly what Rosa feared.

"What kind of mission are we helping out with?" Loco spoke up.

"We hope it's going to lead to a drug bust that's being orchestrated by Easi Ortega."

"Oh boy." Loco shuddered.

"We've got intel that he's hired someone to dump drugs near a private beach. We want aerial footage and eye-witness statements of whatever we find," Rosa explained.

"Do you think, if we get this guy, he'll talk?" Arnold asked.

"I hope so," Rosa continued. "In order to get him I've acquired two boats to intervene if he's spotted and tries to make a break for it. They will just be a couple of fishing boats off in the distance."

"Sounds chancy," Arnold said.

"Why not just bring a sniper?" Loco wondered.

"Well, that's exactly what you will be using until your guns clear through customs. However, I want him alive." She glared at Santos quickly and then looked back at the road.

"When they resist, I shoot," Santos shrugged.

"That's a terrible motto to live by," Arnold said.

"It's different here than in Texas." Santos looked over his shoulder and smiled.

"Yeehaw," Arnold scoffed.

***

The day wore on as Hank brought the customers to their desired location. Maurice was especially diligent in the excursion. He would not waste time. Everyone knew this but no one objected. There was a faint sense of domination about him, as if he had to be in charge.

"You're looking beautiful!" Maurice smiled widely.

Ginny and Josh were being photographed from every angle by Patrick. Their glistening, oiled bodies rubbed against each other, and their bright smiles brought about a cheery sense that was anything but akin to the real world. Patrick could tell Ginny was uncomfortable as Josh copped several feels on her rump rear.

He knew it was not his place to say anything, but he could only take so much.

"Now kiss!" Maurice shouted excitedly.

Josh was about to do just that when Ginny pulled away. "Excuse me?" she asked.

The appalled look of shock on her face was evident.

"You heard me! The magazines will love it!" Maurice cheered.

"Since when do fashion magazines show people making out on them?" Patrick inquired.

"Thank you!" Ginny agreed. "You know, Maurice, this is sounding more and more like your own personal fantasy."

"What're you driving at?" Maurice chuckled nervously.

"You keep making demands that are a bit out of left field. Now this," Ginny stated.

"C'mon, let's give 'em something for the catalogue." Josh smiled. "Maybe we'll start a trend." He leaned forward again.

Ginny fought to resist, placing a hand on his chest to try and push him away.

"Hey, man," Patrick protested.

"Hey what?" Josh pulled away a few inches and glared at the cameraman.

Patrick almost shrank back. Feeling his anger rising, he stood his ground. "Knock it off."

Josh laughed. "Or what?"

"Or I'll have you thrown off my boat!" Hank shouted from above.

He was standing on the upper deck, looking down. Then, Rusty came walking out of the cabin. He was holding a wrench tightly.

"What is happening here?" Maurice stepped between them. "We're just having a bit of fun."

"This isn't a party trip," Hank explained. "You came out here so you could do a photoshoot. Remember, no pornography on my boat. That also includes no sexual assault with or without a camera around."

"I can't believe this!" Maurice threw his hands up over his head. "All I wanted was them to kiss."

"Bullshit," Hank said sternly.

The sky was a bright orange as the sun's rays reached out. Maurice took notice. "I guess we could head back early today. I've got enough here to work with tonight."

His false smile worried Hank. "Alright. I'll bring you back in."

He started the engine and steered the boat towards shore.

Ginny walked away from Josh who stood there agitated.

I'll have you. No one makes a fool of Joshua Rove, he seethed.

Patrick climbed up the ladder and stood near the console. "Thanks."

"No problem," Hank said.

They remained silent momentarily.

"I wouldn't have been able to handle it alone."

"You did alright."

"Really? I thought I could have done more."

"Sometimes, just calling someone out is enough to make them uncomfortable," Hank explained.

"True," Patrick continued. "You know, I'm actually pretty good with boats."

"Oh?" Hank said with feign interest.

"My dad used to drive a boat like this one. We would do charters and I would be his first mate. It was always so much fun. I learned a lot about boats that way."

"Sounds nice," Hank groaned.

"Is something wrong?" Patrick inquired.

"No. I'm fine. Just agitated by what happened, is all."

"I don't blame you." Patrick smiled.

Hank turned to him. "You and Ginny can stay on the Sun Chaser tonight if you want. You two are welcome."

"I'll ask her." Patrick got excited but tried not to let it show.

"Ask me what?" Ginny was halfway up the ladder when the idea was mentioned.

"Um, er, Hank here offered for us to stay on the Sun Chaser tonight."

"What about the motel?" she asked.

"Wouldn't you feel safer away from. . ." He glanced down at the deck where Maurice and Josh were talking.

Ginny seemed to have to think about it. "What will they say?"

"Who cares what they think?" Patrick said. "They don't have a say on where you sleep as far as I'm concerned."

She smiled. "That's very thoughtful but I'm not sure Maurice would like it."

"He's not your boyfriend, Ginny. Not only that, but he has no control on what goes on with you," Patrick stated.

Ginny looked down at the deck again. Then back to Hank and Patrick. "Should I bring it up to them?"

"Nah, we'll just casually mention it when we make port," Hank said over his shoulder.

Patrick looked at her. "I'd feel better if you were away from them."

Thinking back to what had just transpired, Ginny found that the idea was a safer bet than spending the night with those pigs. "Alright."

Silence befell the passengers aboard the Sun Chaser all the way back to the mainland. When the boat pulled into the slick, Josh was quick to hop off and make his way down the dock. Maurice struggled a bit but managed to swing himself over the gunwale and onto the wooden planks. He turned and saw that neither Ginny nor Patrick were behind him.

"Hey, come on you two!"

"I'm staying for tonight," Ginny told him from the upper deck.

"What are you talking about? I have two rooms reserved for us. One for me and you and the other for Josh and Patrick."

"I'm staying too," Patrick called down.

"What? No. I need you both to get off the boat pronto. We've already lost an evening shoot and I'm not going to lose any sleep by standing here arguing," Maurice shouted.

"Then go," Patrick suggested.

Josh walked back to them. "What's going on?"

"These two love birds think they're going to sleep here tonight," Maurice scoffed.

"What? Aboard the boat?" Josh inquired.

Maurice nodded angrily.

"That's a laugh," Josh smirked.

"Look, I'm going to come out and say it," Ginny began. "After the stunt you pulled, I don't feel comfortable with either of you. Please respect my wishes."

Maurice wanted to argue, to say that he had already spent the money on the rooms but realized that he and Josh were in separate rooms regardless of bunk mates. "We'll be back here at the ass crack of dawn. You two had better be ready."

He then stormed off. Josh jogged after him.

"You two can stay in the cabin below tonight. Rusty and I will remain on the upper deck," Hank offered.

"I'll stay on the deck," Patrick said and then turned to Ginny. "I'm sure you want your privacy."

"No, it's okay. I insist." She placed a hand on his shoulder.

"Ok." He smiled.

"There are blankets and pillows in the cubby under the cushion seats." Hank nodded. "We're going to wrap things up, maybe order something to eat. You two hungry?"

"I'm starved," Ginny said.

"What're you guys in the mood for?"

"How about grinders?" she suggested.

"Great! I know a place that sells the best ones around. Do you guys want a six inch or foot long?"

Ginny looked at Patrick and gave him a once over. "I'm sure we can share a foot long."

The innuendo was obvious, and Hank was about to object.

Rusty tugged on his shoulder. Hank looked at him and understood his expression. *Let the kids have fun.*

"We'll be back in forty-five minutes."

"Don't you have to finish up here?" Patrick said nervously.

"It can wait." Hank winked at him.

He then climbed off the boat with Rusty and the two made their way off the dock.

The two stood there for a good while. A sense of longing overcame Patrick. He knew what Ginny wanted. His shy boy nature was beaming through him like a laser blast. He felt small and insignificant. Then there was the hypocrisy of it all. Ginny did not want to go to the motel for a sexual excursion, so she stayed on the boat for one. Perhaps there was more to it. He began to wonder when Ginny turned to him.

"Do I need to paint a sign on my face?" she chuckled.

"What?" Patrick snapped out of his mental gymnastics.

"Mr. Combs," she said flirtatiously. "Take me to the cabin below."

In that moment, a sense of animal magnetism began to spark within him. He looked her over. She was still in her American flag bikini. Her long, blonde hair hung low with beautiful, crumpled curls. She wore an award-winning smile with dazzling blue eyes. Her tanned figure was one of perfection.

She held out her hand and he instinctively took it.

They made their way down the couple of steps and into the cabin below. She took his hand and placed it on her face. His palm cupped it, and she began to kiss it tenderly.

"You're my hero," she said in between pecks.

"Well, I, um…"

"Shh, don't talk." She took his hand again and ushered him over towards the cushioned seats.

CHAPTER SEVEN

The trip of a lifetime.

Anita Torres had fallen in love with her man all over again. They had started dating during their high school years. He was the jock with a heart of gold. She was the shy nerdy girl with braces. Neither saw anything in one another until the senior prom in 1980. Anita's mother had made her go to the event and dolled her up. She couldn't believe how beautiful she looked.

Miguel Ruben had been awestruck at the sight of her. He asked the nervous girl for a dance which turned into several throughout the night. They were glued to each other ever since.

Both living in Mexico City, they dreamed of visiting the ocean. The nearest beach was nearly two hundred miles away at Tecolutla, Verácruz. They had set their sights on a small island off the coast named Leyenda. They saved their money and took scuba diving lessons to explore the coral reefs near there. Neither had brushed up on the local stories to save for surprises when they would arrive.

It was now July 3rd, 1985. Their plane had touched down yesterday, and they had checked into a hotel on the coast of the island. They were now on the shore, making their way to the waterline, to test out their scuba diving gear.

The afternoon sea covered their feet in a lukewarm embrace. It went up to their hips, then their chests. They soon found themselves submerged underwater. Regulators in their mouths, tanks on their backs, everything seemed to be functioning perfectly. The oceanic view became clearer the further they went out. It was teeming with fish and an assortment of colorful rocks. Reds, oranges, and darker blues peppered the sea floor. A light current stirred up a faint sand cloud. The bottom was alive with life and stone.

Hugging the coastline, they made sure not to invade on any property. It was a thought both kept in mind while getting lost in saltwater paradise. Still, Miguel couldn't help but remember something that wasn't too far from their location. He made his way over to Anita and tapped her shoulder. Then, he gestured for her to surface. She looked at him curiously but decided to follow him up.

They surfaced and Miguel turned to her. "I have a great spot we can go to!"

"What do you mean?"

"There's an underwater power line on the bottom about five hundred yards that way." He pointed to his left.

"How would you know that?"

He looked sheepishly at her.

"I thought we agreed on no research!" she shouted.

"It has nothing to do with the local legends, Chica. It's just a place we can visit."

"Why would I want to see a power line?"

"Because, babe, sharks are attracted to the electrical current running through it. Sometimes they even bite into it. We could find shark teeth."

The statement clearly piqued Anita's interest. She looked to where he was pointing again. "Isn't that someone's property?"

"No one will see us. We're not sticking out like a sore thumb on a boat." He laughed heartily.

"Well, alright. We can go."

He kissed her on the cheek. "Thanks, babe."

They put their regulators back in their mouths and dove again.

The water seemed less inviting the more they approached the private area of the water. Nothing visibly changed but Anita couldn't help feeling unwelcome. She knew she was trespassing, and it did not sit right with her. They were in open water. Gaging how far they were from shore by the depth they were currently at, she realized they were only three hundred yards from the beach at most. Anyone from a high vantage point in the hotels would be able to see them.

She began to inch closer to Miguel. It was time to head back. Just then, he stopped. Anita watched as he hung there in the water. Ahead of him was the power line. It was not as he described. There were seemingly no electrical currents running through it judging by the huge gaping hole on its side. It dawned on her in that moment that it wouldn't even make sense to have a power line so close to a beach. It was there though.

Miguel dove down. She faithfully followed. Upon closer inspection they both saw a tubing that ran in conjunction with the power line. They realized exactly what it was. It was a filtration unit that led to the shore. Clear tubing ran along the ocean floor. It was covered in barnacles and moss, but it was clear, nevertheless. Inside it were bags that appeared to contain a white powdery substance.

They both hung there in silence, realizing that the power line was a front for a drug operation. It made sense though. No one would be diving in the area. Miguel began to wonder why even mention a power line in the area anyway if no one was around to see it. He turned to Anita and shrugged. She had a growing look of concern on her face. He tried to calm her by showing how relaxed he was. He took a deep breath and then exhaled. She did the same. Then, he began to reach for her.

Hair came up first, followed by a head with empty eye sockets. The further the corpse rose, the more gruesome details they both saw. She was torn apart and was rising between them. Anita backed away and screamed, almost losing her mouthpiece in the process. Miguel tried to maneuver around the corpse. Every time he tried to move though, she seemed to follow. It wasn't until he looked down and saw a flap of her disemboweled belly was caught on his dive belt, that he too screamed.

She was hanging onto him as if they were performing an interpretive dance. He tried to push her away but only managed to get his fingers caught in her tangled hair. He could feel her pruned scalp and was overcome with nausea.

Anita looked at the scene unfolding. She was hyperventilating. It was so morbid. The woman had been pregnant. Her stretched stomach, namely the marks, made it evident. She had no choice but to pull the regulator out. When she did so, chunks of bile were expelled from her mouth. She then looked at it as the substance rose, and one word came to mind. *Chum.*

Quickly snapping out of her vomit trance, she looked at Miguel. She had to help him. There was no other way around it. She managed to muster the strength and courage to pry her man away from the corpse when, suddenly, a massive shape plowed upward past her. She spun around, lost in a haze of bubbles and flesh. When she regained her bearings, she saw that both the woman and Miguel were gone.

***

"I don't like it any more than you do." Rosa paced back and forth as she spoke over her radio. "It has to be done though."

Arnold sat in the car silently, waiting for the discussion to end. Arnold observed her fit figure barely concealed by her tight white shirt. She wore a black blazer over top and matching color bell bottoms. All the while, her sharp face brought out her stricter demeanor. She was a professional with eye-catching good looks.

She suddenly lowered the radio to her side and made her way back into the police car.

"So, what about our big guns?" Loco smiled.

"Customs will take at least forty-eight hours to clear them. There's nothing I can do about it," she sighed.

Loco and Santos had been arguing the whole time. They placed bets on who would nail the kill shot on Easi if given the opportunity. Now it was all for nothing.

"He could be halfway across Mexico by that time!" Loco cried out.

"Let's just scope the area out. Hopefully their dumper will make a move tonight."

"If he doesn't?" Arnold questioned.

"Then we'll need to resort to another strategy."

"Listen. No offense, Rosa, but me and Loco have a store to run. Even if the weapons were cleared in less than forty-eight hours, we weren't planning on staying here for more than a couple of days," Arnold stated.

"This is a big job, Arnie," Rosa began. "You and Loco knew damn well of that. It could take a week even if everything went to plan and that's being generous. No, we need you here. Besides, I just got off the horn with the chief, he's offering to pay you a thousand dollars each for your services. If we succeed, he'll double that."

Both men sat back in their seats. It wasn't a relatively high figure, but it would be enough to keep the store closed for at least another day or two more.

"We leave on the fifth unless we are close to being successful," Arnold said.

"What about the fireworks show?" Loco glared at his boss.

"They'll make it one year without us," Arnold said. "Besides, I promise a fireworks show tomorrow. They all explode the same no matter where they are set off."

"Alright. It's a deal," Rosa said. "We'll head to the beach house where the dumper was spotted last and you two be on standby with that chopper. We may be in for a long night."

***

Smoke flowed in the air as the man took a hit of his cigarette alone in the hotel room. A collective ball of nicotine, it eventually disappeared only for it to be replaced by another puff of carbon-monoxide gas. The producer of the chemical substance lay backwards slightly on the sun chair and watched as the sun's rays danced along the sky.

Maurice was in the next room over, also on the patio. Their two rooms were practically conjoined, only separated by a door inside that was held closed by a chair on both sides. He was sipping on a gin and tonic. He occasionally looked to his right and saw Josh smoking like his lungs depended on it.

"You aggravated too?" Maurice wondered.

Josh pulled the cigarette from his lips with a popping sound and then inhaled through his teeth. "I just don't get it. We didn't do anything wrong."

"She's just being a prude."

"Oh yeah!" Josh exclaimed. "One hundred percent."

The two sat there watching as the sun dipped further behind the horizon.

"I have an idea for tomorrow."

"Oh yeah?" Josh inquired.

"Underwater photography."

Josh laughed. "With the dolphin threat out there? Ginny won't go for it, and neither will Patrick or Hank."

"Too bad. I paid for this gig. If I say we're diving tomorrow, then we're diving."

"Interesting," Josh said, bemused. "How do you propose we go diving without swimsuits?"

"More like snorkeling. I purchased some equipment from a gift shop."

"You cheap bastard," Josh chuckled.

"It's my money. I do what I want with it. I'll spend it however I please!"

"Okay, man. No need to get testy." Josh held up his hands defensively.

"Just stop smoking for tonight."

"Why?"

"You may need to use your lungs to their fullest capacity tomorrow."

"Come again?"

"Not all the shots I want will require a mask." He smiled.

"I still don't get where you're going with this but, alright."

He put his cigarette out on the wooden balcony and turned in for the night.

***

Burt Stone had been a fan of the band Journey since the late seventies. He used to jam out to their summer hits and swayed along with their love ballads. When the singer, Steve Perry, pursued a solo album, most thought he was nuts. It would be a death sentence for the band. It was not until last year when he released *Street Talk* that most restored faith in him. Burt never gave up on him though.

The chiming synthesizers blared over his stereo system inside his beachside home. He had been up there for a month trying to get over his divorce and jamming to mournful music. *Oh, Sherrie* was his perfect remedy for the messy break up. His ex-wife's name was Cheryl, and that fact made the song hit even harder.

While Perry's chorus cheered her name, he cried tears of joy. He felt like he was on stage and looking over the crowd, a sea of Cheryls. The climax of the song came, and he began to make his way over to the balcony. The synth chiming began again, and he looked out over the bay as it faded out.

It was a beautiful sight with the lapping waves brushing against the waterline and the vast blue beyond. The song ended and he began to go back into the room when, suddenly, he saw something out in the surf. It was a small mass, like a bundle of items, almost in the shape of a human.

He swiftly made his way out of the room and charged down the stairs. Once outside on the beach, he jogged over to the shoreline. It was clear now it was a woman who had scuba gear on and was holding something.

"Damnit, how many more people are going to be on my property!"

The woman moaned.

"Oh Jesus, get up," he scoffed at her.

She slowly got up. Her legs were aching.

"Far swim from out there, huh?" he chuckled.

He then looked at her closely. She was clearly shaken and afraid. Something had happened to her. She then held her hands out and he saw what she was holding. It was a severed head.

"It ate them!" she screamed suddenly.

CHAPTER EIGHT

His night was set.

Easi Ortega observed the television from his couch with a kind of moth-to-flame interest. Something about the pigmented lights that conjoined to make a whole image suddenly fascinated him. It was beyond all rationale. He was experiencing a world not unlike their own and yet it was. The distant future of 2019 was presented as a cold, wet, desolate place with plenty of bright lights and yet no real color.

His face was inches from the tube. He couldn't care less what it did to his eyes. There was nothing that could draw him away from it as he watched a poor-qualify version of *Blade Runner*. Despite the resolution, the visual experience was still one to admire. He watched as Harrison Ford was driven to the Tyrell Corporation in a trippy sequence involving a flying car called a Spinner towards a building with an abundance of tiny lights that were, in fact, windows. The Vangeles score drove his mind wired as he sniffed a pencil-length of cocaine off his arm.

Suddenly, there was a knock on his doorframe. He turned and saw a woman standing there. She was not Mexican but was Caucasian and beautiful, nevertheless.

"Can I come in?"

He nearly pinched himself. Was he dreaming or was this a set up by Sofia to test his loyalty? Then he saw Rafael and Philipe standing behind her. There was no doubt that who he was seeing was real and that it was not a dream.

"Who are you?"

"Let's just say, I have connections that you are going to need. I mean, if you want to keep this operation running, that is." She gave a sly grin.

Easi nodded and she entered the room. Rafael and Philipe stood by the door.

"This is a private matter, Mr. Ortega." She glanced over her shoulder.

"They are my two most trustworthy goons. Whatever you have to say, they should be privy to it, Ms..."

"Morgan, Ollie Morgan," she stated.

"Aren't you related to Lewis Morgan, the construction operator?"

"He's my husband." She smiled.

Easi scratched his chin and then rubbed his nose. "What could you possibly have to offer me and my crew?"

"The mayor can get people off your back."

"How so?"

"He's my brother. He'll do almost anything I say."

"Interesting." Easi got off his recliner and made his way over to her. "How much?"

"We don't need money. We've got plenty," Ollie said.

"Then what is it you do need?"

She stalled for a moment. "It's these dolphins."

"Dolphins?" Easi inquired.

"Yes. They will cause trouble for our beaches. A pregnant woman was attacked and killed."

"When was this?"

"This morning."

"Why didn't I hear about it on the news?" Easi wondered.

"Believe me, the husband and the family that saw the attack were desperate to have it reach the press' ears."

"You silenced them?"

"They're alive, if that's what you're getting at."

"Never said they weren't."

"Anyway, the family and husband of the pregnant woman made their way around town and spread the word. That was a couple of hours ago. Already, the news is encroaching on the story. Nothing official. Not yet at least."

Philipe and Rafael observed from the doorway; the tension in the room was growing.

"How do you want us to go about taking care of a couple of dolphins?"

"Apparently there are four," Ollie corrected him.

"Two, four, ten. Who cares, really? I can get rid of them. I just want the police and mayor off our backs."

"You have a guy. He dumps drugs for you. I want you to have him pose as a charter captain. When he goes out with some customers, have him dump poison into the water," Ollie explained.

"What if the tourists don't want to go where the dolphins are?"

"It's a big ocean. I don't think one detour would throw them off."

"If you say so," Easi sighed. "I still don't think you're telling me the whole truth."

"I guarantee I can get the police and mayor off your back for a while. At least long enough to finish up your operations here."

"That may take a while. We kind of like it here." Easi smiled.

"How long?"

"A year, two? We're very successful in this area. Maybe throw in some passports to America after we're done?"

"Deal."

"Alright." Easi watched as Ollie turned and began back towards the doorway. "Oh, and Mr. Ortega. Watch out for sharks."

He looked at her questioningly. "Swindlers, buisnessmen, what sharks are you talking about?"

"The kind that have stripes," she said.

"El demonio rayado?"

"The very same."

"He's just a legend."

"For your sake and mine, I hope you're right," she said.

As she turned, she stared at Rafael and Philipe who didn't utter a word. There was an obvious chain of power in the room and Ollie knew that, in the moment, she was on top.

***

The night wore on as Lewis stared into his bottle of beer. He nursed it back and then returned to stare at the grandfather clock positioned on the mantle above the fireplace. There was a stiffness in the air that smelled of old people. He knew Eddie and Ollie's parents were bed ridden before they died but he did not expect the smell to linger long after they were gone.

To his right on an old rocking chair sat Eddie. He never seemed to mind the atrocious accumulation of flaky flesh. He reveled in their absence. It not only helped him financially, but it boosted his political career and placed him more in the public eye.

Lewis got up and approached the balcony. He opened the glass doors and then turned to make his way back to the out-of-style couch he had gotten mildly comfortable in.

"Shut the doors if you're not going outside."

"It reeks in here."

"You've been saying that for months."

"Yeah, and it hasn't gotten any better," Lewis protested.

"Then go outside."

Lewis turned and shut the doors and stormed across the living room. He made his way to the front doors.

"Where are you going?"

"For a drive."

"Hopefully you don't see any more bums eaten by sharks," he chuckled.

He ignored him and opened the door where he jumped out of his skin.

"Ollie! You scared the shit out of me," Lewis said, trying to recover from the temporary shock.

She stood there, oblivious to his shaken figure. "No need to be afraid. I've taken care of everything."

"Oh?" Eddie looked at her, intrigued.

"Yep. I've solved our little dolphin problem."

"You don't really think dolphins are the problem, do you?"

"Lewis, darling, I believe you saw a collective dolphin attack. The water must have made it seem like a flow of teeth and stripes."

"I saw more than that. The shark was massive."

"Dolphins creating a ruckus can make quite the splash." She smiled.

Lewis shook his head.

"It doesn't matter. We need to focus on the task at hand. I've got an infestation."

"Don't you mean a finfestation." Eddie grinned.

"Shut up, big brother. I hired some people to take care of it."

"Who? It's not Jose's people, is it?"

"No, you don't know them personally," Ollie said as she made her way to the fireplace.

As she casually placed her hand on the mantle, she remained silent. Deep in thought and yet attentive to her surroundings. She placed a finger atop the grandfather clock and wiped it.

"Place is in need of dusting."

"Who did you hire?" Eddie inquired again.

"With a good sweep we could get rid of this pesky filth." She smiled.

Eddie remained silent.

"If you won't tell us, then why even bring it up?" Lewis chimed in.

"In time you'll know. Now is not that time."

Eddie shot out of his rocking chair. "I demand you tell me who and how much you spent on them!"

"It won't cost you a dime, big brother." She remained calm.

"Oh really?" he said sarcastically.

"You are over exaggerating. Will you two let me handle this problem my way?"

"As long as the beaches are open and safe tomorrow that's all I care about," Eddie stated.

"By tomorrow you'll wish you had thought of it sooner." She winked and made her way towards the stairs.

"Where do you think you're going?" Lewis asked.

"To bed, you comin'?"

"I'm not satisfied."

"Well, I can satisfy you in other ways, darlin'."

"Somehow I don't believe you can tonight."

"Baby, I didn't sit outside to get this tan for the seagulls." She gently placed a hand against her thigh. "I'll only ask one more time. I'm feeling frisky tonight. You comin'?"

"Please don't say that shit in front of me," Eddie said.

"Then turn on some music." Ollie smiled and then held her hand out.

Lewis waited momentarily but eventually decided to take it. She led him upstairs as Eddie got up and made his way to his record player. He quickly searched for a vinyl and decided on one by a British band called Night. He put it on the device and placed the needle on its grooved surface. A cover of Walter Egan's *Hot Summer Nights* began to play. It seemed fitting given the overly warm time of day it was. As Stevie Lange sang, her voice melted his soul. He always had a thing for her unique voice. Her range had no bounds.

After a while, he began to doze off. He was thankful he did so before the chandelier above him began to sway.

***

They were listening as Lee Cortez made his way up and down the beach shouting. He was going ballistic on anyone that would listen. His insistence on spreading the word was becoming both an irritation and sorrowful. The small group of people that were on the beach felt bad for him. There hadn't been a shark attack in around ten years. As far as people were concerned, the man was crazy. *It killed my wife and unborn son.*

Some were watching him from afar. The dune buggy was parked in a small patch of grass before the white sand began. The two pairs of eyes had been following him up and down the beach for an hour. Now, as the crowd thinned out even further, it was time to plan.

"Rafael, she didn't say anything about a cover up," Philipe stated.

"No, but Easi wants a clean story. He won't settle for a surprise twist."

"Let's just leave him be. The guy has suffered enough, don't ya think?"

"He wants revenge on a fish. I say he's still got plenty of piss and vinegar in him."

"You think he will dig?"

"All the way to China if he has to." Rafael turned to him. "Easi has a theory on why the dolphins are going crazy. He thinks they ingested some of the Coke 2.0."

"Oh fuck. We have to cover this up, man." Philipe looked around wide eyed.

"Exactly." Rafael turned back to the raving man on the beach. "Say. Let's take our friend here for a little boat ride. All expenses paid," he chuckled.

Philipe sat there, quietly. "Is there another way?"

"I don't think he'll take a bribe," Rafael sighed. "I'm sure Easi would have rather that be his first option."

"So what do we do?"

"Capture."

"No release?"

"No release," Rafael repeated, answering his partner's question.

The two wasted no time climbing out of the dune buggy. Rafael reached under his seat and produced a tranquilizer pistol with a silencer on it. Casually, the two walked down to the beach.

Lee almost immediately saw them and began to panic. "I'm not hurting anyone!"

"No," Rafael raised the weapon. "But we are."

Before Lee had time to react, a dart entered his skin.

Philipe kept an eye out. No one was around close enough to get a good idea of what they were doing. Nor were they even looking in their direction, deliberately ignoring the wild-eyed man.

They scooped him up and hustled back to the dune buggy. Soon, he was stuffed into the backseat. It was cramped but he wouldn't care. Rafael and Philipe then hopped in the front and tore off across the dunes. The vehicle bounced around as if it were hitting every pothole on a beaten road.

When they arrived at Easi's private dock, there was a single boat there. It was a pristine, turbo engined, speedboat. There was a compartment for bait and tackle as well as a metal box for supplies. There was a beautiful windowpane near the steering wheel that was eye level with the driver. The dashboard was made out of ebony wood and varnish coated. It was cleaned daily by Easi who didn't seem to mind the labor. Sofia had begun to wonder if he was spending more time ogling the tiny boat than her.

Rafael sat Lee down on the seat next to him as he took on the console chair. Philipe was kneeling on the dock, untying the rope from the cleat. When he gave the go ahead, he hopped on the boat just as Rafael eased on the throttle.

The night air was refreshing after such a miserably humid day. Stars covered the sky in a showcase of dazzling dots. Philipe stared up, swearing he saw some of them pulsating like a rhythmic heartbeat. It worried him at first but, soon, it became a numbing viewing experience. He could practically hear the drum beat in his head.

"Dude! Wake up!" Rafael shouted.

Philipe snapped out of it. The boat was stopped. He looked around and saw that the shoreline was a small veil on the horizion. It ran across it and seemed to never end.

"Help me get this guy up," Rafael ordered.

Looking down at the gagged, sweaty man, he began to feel bad again. "C'mon, man."

"Do I have to make you help me?" Rafael screamed.

Taken aback, Philipe quickly collected himself to not show fear. He placed his arms under the man's armpits and hefted him up onto his feet.

"There's no need to try and scream. It will be useless." Rafael smiled as he reached for the man.

With a quick yank, the cloth came free of his mouth. The man coughed and gagged but soon found himself sobbing. "She was my everything."

"If you keep screaming about dolphins killing your wife, you'll find that people will do just about anything to know why," Rafael chuckled.

"Dolphins? What are you talking about?"

"I'm talking about predator mammals that are acting crazy. I'm talking about the pod of them that killed your wife and unborn child." Rafael did not hide his devilish grin.

"You dumb bastards!" Lee laughed. "You're just like the doctors and investigators. My wife was killed by a shark."

"A shark?" Philipe asked, interest piqued.

"A big shark. A bus with teeth!"

"I'd argue dolphins are more dangerous," Rafael stated.

"You're wrong," Lee scowled. "It was the biggest fish I have ever seen."

"The family didn't seem to think so," Rafael said nonchalantly.

"How did you know about the family?"

"Let's just say I paid them a little visit earlier today," Rafael stated.

Philipe looked at him, disgusted. He remained silent though. Despite them being friends, he still feared the man.

Rafael reached down and unholstered his glock. He then pointed it at Lee's head.

Bang.

His partner jumped as the bullet exited the weapon and smashed into Lee's skull. There were no last words allowed. No remorse. No mercy.

"Let's get back to shore. I'm in the mood for some seafood," Rafael chuckled.

"What about him?" Philipe pointed to the dead man.

He was slumped over, his cranium pulsating blood in a rhythm that reminded Philipe of the stars above.

Grabbing the man by his legs, Rafael hoisted his lower body up and then managed to toss him overboard.

"Now he'll have some seafood too." He gave a hearty laugh.

CHAPTER NINE

A bleak outlook.

The night wore on like a bad dream. Quinn sat on the Bow Dipper, a bottle of beer in one hand and a cigarette in the other. The alcohol was almost gone and his source of nicotine was down to the butt, smoldering away like his life choices. He bellowed out a yawn that would make a lion blush. It was almost midnight. He got out of the fishing chair and began to make his way below deck when he heard a faint droning noise. It was almost like a buzzing sound.

When he turned to investigate, a blinding light aimed at his face.

He shielded his eyes and squinted, forcing himself to look. There, on a speedboat, were two men. They looked all too familiar.

"Now what is it you want?" Quinn shouted.

"It isn't a matter of what we want," Rafael chuckled and placed a hand on the gunwale. "How's the hand?"

"It will heal. Unlike what I'll do to your faces if you don't tell me what it is you're both doing here at this time of night!"

"Someone's testy, ay pal?" Rafael turned to Philipe who seemed disinterested.

"Can you take that light off me?" Quinn asked.

Rafael lowered the searchlight and turned it off.

It took a few seconds before Quinn's eyes were able to adjust back to the darkness. "For the final time, what do you want?"

"Easi made it clear to us that we are to accompany you tomorrow."

"What? Why?"

"There has been a slight change in plans."

"Oh?" Quinn wondered.

"We have a dolphin problem. They attacked and killed a woman. The mayor wants them gone and has hired us to hunt them down and take care of them."

Quinn suppressed a laugh. "You two can't handle some dolphins by yourselves?"

"There is good reason to believe they've been affected by Coke 2.0."

"Nonsense. I drop them secured. There hasn't been any leakage."

"As far as you know. Maybe one of the bags got loose and they took it in," Rafael explained.

"Highly unlikely."

"But not impossible." Rafael stared at him. "We have to be sure, and we have to clean this mess up."

"How do you suppose we do that?"

"We'll drop poison into the water. It'll be all sneaky like." Rafael held up a bag. "Lead poisoning."

"You may contaminate the waters for a while doing that."

"You got a better option?" Philipe argued.

Quinn looked to him, surprised to hear they would let him come up with something. "I can trick them to the surface and shoot them with a shark gun."

"Too many witnesses."

"Witnesses? What witnesses?"

"We need to have someone charter the boat to make it look inconspicuous. No one would suspect a boat full of rowdy tourists."

Quinn laughed aloud. "That's really dumb. And what about them? When they see what we do.. ."

"They won't," Rafael said, trying to reassure him.

"This is crap. I don't like it."

"You don't have much of a choice," Rafael said.

Barely able to clench his left fist, Quinn realized the goon was right. "So who are our unlucky tourists?"

"Scope out the harbor tomorrow morning. If they want a ride, we'll give it to them. First come first served." Rafael smiled like the Cheshire cat from *Alice in Wonderland.*

"I'm sure we'll have a wonderful time," Quinn groaned.

***

Hank awoke from a nightmare. He did not often have them. Facing away from the window, he turned to look out into the starry night sky. He could hear the waves lapping against the shoreline and the chirping of crickets with insomnia apparently. The incessant stridulation was getting on his nerves quickly and he got up.

As he gazed out, he saw a couple of boats near the Stone estate. Leyenda was a rather large island on a small chain. There were plenty of houses on the coast, but Burt Stone always seemed to have bad luck. Hank rubbed his eyes but couldn't see who was out there. He reached over to grab his binoculars from his nightstand but he was too far. He walked over and retrieved them. Once he got back to the window and adjusted them, the two boats were separating from each other.

"What the heck?" Hank sighed.

He had trouble getting the binoculars to focus as the speedboat sped out of there so he directed them back to the fishing boat they were near. He quickly recognized it as Quinn's boat, the Bow Dipper. He had always laughed at the name but, lately, he started thinking that maybe Quinn wanted to die at sea. Regardless, the man was there now with a sour expression on his face and a scowl that would make the happiest person frown in response.

Quinn then went below to turn in for the night.

Lowering the binoculars by his side, Hank tried to recall what the nightmare was about. He always forgot them when he woke up but this time it seemed important. It was almost as if it were a premonition.

"Oh Rusty," he sulked.

He didn't know why he said his first mate's name, but he felt a heavy weight on his chest. It would do him the world to call him but that was not a possibility for the mute man. Hank shrugged to himself and crawled back into bed. He placed the binoculars on his bedside table and dozed off.

***

Rosa always resented being at home. She felt she never accomplished anything while there. Tonight was different though. She had company. Arnold Ray sat across the table from her with a plateful of spaghetti and a glass of wine in front of him.

He chuckled. "I never figured you for the Italian type."

She smirked. "I'm a connoisseur for all things yummy."

The two sat in silence briefly as they consumed some of the long noodles and sipped from their fruity alcoholic beverages.

"Can I ask you something?" Arnold asked.

Rosa wondered where he was going to go with it. Hoping to get him to admit he still had feelings for her, she opened up. "Sure."

"Why this case?"

Leaning back into her wooden chair, she sighed. "It's personal."

"Don't the police generally frown upon officers pursuing conflicts of interest?"

"I'm not close with the guy. I know of him."

"So doesn't the entire island of Leyenda?"

"You just answered your own question."

"How so?" Arnold inquired.

"Everyone's got a score to settle with Easi and his gang."

"So why you?"

"I'm a detective lieutenant. I take any case I damn well want," she stated.

"Interesting."

"Why are you always so nosy?" she shouted.

"There she is." Arnold held his hands out.

"Oh, shut it."

"What are your ties to this gang in particular?"

"Easi killed my father," Rosa was yelling now.

The awkward silence returned momentarily.

"I can't believe you were allowed to take on this case," he said coldly.

"Just do the job I hired you for!" she snarled.

With that, Arnold got up and made his way to the door.

"Where are you going?" she asked.

"Gotta get up early tomorrow. Wouldn't want to be tired while flying a chopper around the island."

She nodded, visibly upset.

Arnold walked back over to her. He placed a finger gently under her chin and raised her head to look into his eyes. "I think we both know why it didn't work out now."

"It was a long time ago."

"Indeed it was. We're just two souls lost in this crazy world."

"Why can't we find each other again?"

"What would it prove?" Arnold asked.

"That even angry couples can work," she giggled.

"Perhaps they're not meant to." He saw a tear fall down her cheek.

He released her and made his way towards the door again.

"Until tomorrow." He smiled and then walked out.

***

The bar was alive with patrons. Bar hopping was a favorite amongst the locals and many were warming themselves up for the festivities over the next couple of days. One man, with a Coors Light in grasp, sat brooding on his barstool. He had been stuffing his face with complementary peanuts for an hour now and the bartender was becoming annoyed.

"A bit egregious, no?" He looked down at the bowl.

"Can I just enjoy myself in peace?" the man asked.

"I don't see why not. Just go easy on the peanuts please."

The two men shared a nod.

Across the room at a table, a foot tapped to the song on the radio, *I'm Still Standing* by Elton John. The fun doo wop had the establishment hopping as people in the center danced their hearts out. The pop song was having an infectious effect on everyone besides the gloomy man sitting at the bar. Santos smiled as he recognized Loco. He casually got up and made his way over, avoiding swaying hips and shaking arms.

He took a seat next to him. "Where's your friend?"

"Getting lucky, what's it to ya?" Loco snapped at him.

"Oh, that's right. Our illustrious lieutenant was getting quite lonely with me."

"Why would she?" Loco asked, only half interested.

"I'm gay," Santos said flatly.

"I see." Loco nodded. "So, tell me Small Boat, suck any good ones lately?"

"Don't call me small boat." He took a deep breath. "Not that it's any of your business but I'm not into that kind of stuff."

"Well, that's too bad. Maybe the deli will offer you a free sausage at the market."

"Fuck you," Santos snapped.

Loco didn't respond.

"You know what bothers me about you two. You and Arnold came to help but there must be a catch. There always has to be a catch!" Santos was screaming now.

"We're being paid," Loco grumbled.

"Bullshit. You know Arnie-boy is coming to sweep Rosa off her feet."

"What do you care? You're gay," Loco reiterated.

Santos' face was a beet red Loco had never seen on a man before. "Take a chill pill, man."

"I care about her wellbeing," Santos growled.

"Look, Arnold's not a bad guy."

"Then why did he leave the lieutenant high and dry?"

"His reasons are his own," Loco said softly.

He hoped the altercation would not escalate further. He didn't need to kick this prick's teeth in. In all honesty, he did not want to. Loco could smell the alcohol on him and knew a drunk cop was not something to trifle with.

"Listen, pal. I want to know what your intentions are," Santos demanded, placing a hand on the man's shoulder.

Loco shrugged it off, letting the hand slide from him. "I'm just a good friend doing my good deed for the year."

"Uh huh. Well, keep it up, good Samaritan. We'll see who has the last laugh."

Santos then pushed away from the bar and made his way back to his table. Loco exhaled and looked at the bartender who seemed to want to throw them both out. "More peanuts please."

***

Anita Ruben awkwardly rose from the sea. She did not want to live anymore. The constant threat of being stalked on land and in the sea was too much to bear. Enough was enough. There was a hit on her head for what she had seen. A man had been following her all day.

If she were to die it would be by her own desire.

She waded further into the ocean, water brushing against her bare chest. The shark was out there somewhere. It would be only fitting to be killed by what had taken her husband. In her mind, there was no other way. To her it was ironic in a way to be devoured by a fish. She respected the sea and would now be consumed by it.

Soon she was backstroking. She was near the net that kept sharks out. There was no more time to contemplate. Lifting one hand out of the water and placing it on the net, she clumsily swung over it. She almost laughed as she imagined how she must have looked. Anita then righted herself and began to tread water again.

"I'll be with you soon, Miguel," she spoke up to the star-filled sky.

Terrified yet smiling, she felt crossing over the net was a jump into unfamiliar waters. The threshold gone, the barrier broken. She was now victim to whatever lay beyond it. Part of her wanted to turn back but she fought against it.

Splash.

The sound came from her left. Her eyes darted towards its direction. There were more splashes off in the distance. They sounded like something was slicing through the water while slapping its tail against it. The water suddenly became choppy. It lapsed against her, causing her to go with the flow and lose her sense of direction.

A faint sound was then heard.

Eee eee eee eee.

Dolphins? she wondered.

The pod had sensed a disturbance in the ocean ever since the drug was lowered into it. After witnessing the massive shark consume one of the bags, things had only gotten worse. The shark had claimed lives and was a menace to the sea and its inhabitants.

Their sonar had pinpointed its location. It was near a net, swimming back and forth as if it were waiting for something, or someone. Much like the killer whale was a menace to seals, nets were a perfect way to incapacitate and drown them. There was something else though, a wrench in their plan to kill it. Their sonar had also picked up a human life form.

When the great beast made its way to the west side of the net, they approached from the east. They had to warn this female to leave. By the time they got her attention, it was on its way back.

Anita sensed something was wrong. The dolphins were calling to her but were keeping their distance. They were deathly afraid of something. There was a force not to be trifled with nearby. Even they could not help her.

A new sensation came over her. She felt an overwhelming desire to face her attacker. She had not gotten a good look at the shark and knew nothing about it other than it was massive. She felt content enough to duck her head under the water and open her eyes. The salt stung briefly but, when her eyes adjusted, she saw nothing. She turned to her right and saw it. There it was, a gargantuan goliath.

A tiger shark.

She could not muster up the courage to scream. She only stared as it quickened its approach.

The sway of its caudal fin would be enough to break bone, the skin, covered in some strange kind of barnacle, could scrape skin off of flesh. There was no undermining the jaws. When they parted to filter water through its gills, the gap was already eight inches. If she were to determine, the shark's jaws would have to be three feet wide.

For some reason that terrified her further, the shark was not picking up speed. Instead, it kept at a steady pace, casually closing the distance. Although Anita wanted to die, it was frightening to see her killer's features as it spent an eternity approaching to attack her.

Five feet separated them now.

Eee eee eee eee.

The dolphins were in an uproar. The shark was almost stationary. It seemed to relish in her fear and anguish. Then, the jaws hyper extended and she was sucked into its mouth. The rush of water carried her down its gullet.

She was gone but not dead. She would not be for a few minutes until she either drowned in the water or burned in its stomach acid.

CHAPTER TEN

Dawn broke over the glassy surface.

Boats, nestled in their slicks, creaked as they teetered side to side. Water gently lapsed against the hulls creating a deep, hollow sound. They were old souls trapped in fiberglass and wood vessels. Sailors and fishermen felt a connection to these haunting creations that were of scientific engineering.

They remained where they were by ropes tied to cleats. The docks were home to an assortment of life. Some portions were slightly rotted due to sea termites chewing plank by plank. Their progression was somewhat hampered by pesticides which were routinely sprayed.

Crustaceans crawled up the pilings and would pick at the tiny insects. A nuisance for humans, a feast for them. The water was still. The crabs could cling to the docks for hours and not be disturbed by splashes that would knock them off.

Life was treated by a ranking order. They were both infesting the docks but for different reasons. One wanted to devour manmade creations while, the other, wanted a natural food source.

One crab made its way onto the dock itself. It immediately became disorientated. Lost in a foreign area. Soon, it began to scurry across. It was not too dissimilar to a fly pressed against a window. Both yearned for an attractive lure of sorts.

In the crab's case it was some scraps that were left behind. The crustacean was quick to snatch the aluminum foil-covered food and began to pick at it with its free claw.

Woosh.

To the creature, it felt like it had been hit by a figurative train. Wind blew past its shell as it was flown away. There was no sense of loss or regret. Survival instincts set in, and it managed to free one appendage.

It pinched the seagull on the snout which, in turn, caused the bird to screech and release it. It landed hard on the deck of a boat. The seagull was quick to correct its course and swoop down again.

The crab rose on its hind legs as the seagull landed. Both were locked in a game of speed and wits. The bird lunged forward with frightening force. In doing so, its beak was snagged. The crab had pinched it shut.

"There's something you don't see every day," Patrick chuckled.

Ginny looked up from his chest. She then followed his gaze and saw the scene unfolding before them. The crab had the seagull's beak in a vice-like grip and was shaking its head back and forth.

She giggled.

"She rises." Patrick looked down at her.

"Honestly, I didn't want to."

"Was I that good?"

She smiled and placed her head back down on his chest, nestling against it.

"I take that as a yes."

She moaned in agreement.

A sudden urge came over Patrick and he brushed a hair off to the side of her face. He could not believe how beautiful she was. Her gorgeous golden locks shined as the morning sun began to seep in through the cabin window. He lifted his head forward slightly and kissed the top of hers.

Smiling, she rubbed a hand on his chest. "Want to go again before they get back?"

"No, let's not be rude. I'm sure they'll walk in on us, and it would be awkward," he laughed.

"For Hank and Rusty or Josh and Maurice?"

"Either duo," he chuckled.

Uncoiling herself from him and the blanket that covered them, she made her way across to the bar. Her naked body had a nice bronze tan, and he could not help but admire her.

"Where'd you learn to do that thing?" she asked.

"What thing?" he asked.

"You know, the thing with your tongue."

"Long story. Basically, I had a kinky girlfriend years back. She taught me all sorts of ways to pleasure a woman."

"I hope to learn more of them." She returned with a couple of bottles of water.

She handed one to Patrick and he accepted it. "Thanks."

The two took a sip and then turned to each other.

"Why me?" he inquired.

"What?" she wondered.

"I'm not buff like Josh or sleazy like Maurice."

"Do you think I am solely a muscle and money kind of gal?" she said without an angered tone.

"No. Not at all. I am just surprised, is all."

"How   so?"

"Let me put it into perspective." He nervously smiled.

"Please do." Ginny tilted her head back and drank more water.

"Well, you're like a high school cheerleader while I'm the nerdy tech kid."

"Oh, well. I'll let you in on a little secret, Mr. Combs," she continued. "I was never part of the cheerleading team. I was part of the choir. I was dating a member of the school band back then. We were all nerds. I just happened to   be   one   of   the   prettier   ones."

"So, you find me attractive because I remind you of what you once had?"

"I find you attractive because you're a nice guy. Yes, a bit of it may have to do with nostalgia. Nevertheless, you have a confidence no tech guy in my school ever possessed."

"I guess I ooze cool." He grinned cheekily.

"God, you're such a nerd." She playfully pushed his shoulder.

"You know you love it," he laughed aloud.

"Permission to come aboard, love birds?" Hank called from the dock.

The two turned to each other and couldn't help but giggle like school kids.

"Of course," Patrick replied.

Hank and Rusty climbed aboard.

"Everyone decent?" Hank asked.

Ginny looked down at her naked body and then at Patrick's. "Five minutes please."

The two then got dressed and made their way out onto the deck.

"Any word from Maurice?" Patrick asked.

"I haven't spoken to him since last evening," Hank stated.

"Hopefully they come soon," Ginny said, a little worried that they were running late.

It was not like Maurice to fall behind. Usually, he was right on time or a bit before.

"There they are." Patrick pointed to the shore where the parking lot was.

Both Maurice and Josh made their way down the steps and onto the dock. They were each carrying a backpack. When they got within ear shot, Hank called to them. "What's that you two have got there?"

"A little surprise," Maurice said as he stopped at the Sun Chaser. "Permission to come aboard?"

"Permission granted." Hank held out a hand and grabbed the bags from them.

As the two swung their legs over, Hank was tempted to open the bags. "What's the plan for today?"

"I want to go to the cove," Maurice explained.

"Which one? "Brighten Cove?"

"That spot is reserved for divers."

"Well, I guess we're getting a little wet today," Maurice stated.

Hank stared at him momentarily and held one of the backpacks to his chest. He feverishly unzipped it. Josh moved forward to protest, but Maurice placed his arm out in front of him.

"This was not part of our agreement," Hank said as he held out a pair of goggles.

"We're not diving. Just snorkeling," Maurice smiled pleasantly.

"Did you forget about the dolphins? Or did you just choose to ignore the danger?" Hank was genuinely confused.

"Just take us out there, boat man. We need at least an hour to get the shots. We'll be in and out," Maurice explained.

"Not on my boat," Hank stated. "No way. Under different circumstances, maybe. Not with those crazy dolphins out there though."

"It'll be worth it. I'll pay extra," Maurice argued.

"The answer is still no."

The two were in a standoff. No one interjected with a counter argument. There was no reason to. It was plain and simple.

"You'll be sorry," Maurice snarled and then snatched the backpack from him. "Ginny, Pat. Let's get the hell off this shit heap. It smells anyway."

Patrick wanted to argue but realized it would put his job on the line. Part of him was happy they were staying on shore. The sea was not safe now. He collected his things as Ginny climbed off. He sensed she felt the same way by the look she gave him when she stood on the dock.

"Don't go with this schmuck, kid," Hank argued.

"I have to. It's my job," Patrick said.

"Be careful," he spoke softly. "I don't trust those two."

Patrick nodded and then made his way onto the dock.

Philipe was already starting to regret his decision to come along. The heat of the eighty-six-degree July morning was particularly excruciating. Other annoyances paled in comparison. Not even the persistent seagulls that were swarming the dock or the occasional blaring of a horn to signify departure could top it. The humidity was unbearable.

He reached across the table in the cabin of the Bow Dipper and snatched a half empty can of his beer. That was another thing to add to the list. The boat kept tipping to the left which was opposite the side he was sitting on. His beverage followed suit. He kept muttering under his breath. *Do it, I dare you. Just one more time.*

"Yo, Philly-boy. Come help me get this damn bucket ready." It was Quinn.

The captain was the last person Philipe wanted to talk to at the moment. He begrudgingly got up and made his way to the door. "Where's Rafael?"

"He's busy. I need you, lad."

"Should probably ask me on a date first," Philipe laughed aloud. "I'm not your boat boy."

"No but you are my cabin boy. Get the fuck up here, pronto!" Quinn shouted.

Deciding not to argue about it further, Philipe crawled out of the cabin. The overhang was low, and it made it difficult to get in and out of the section of the boat. The interior was a stark contrast, wide and spacious. He made his way towards Quinn who was having trouble hefting the bucket onto one of the compartments on the starboard side. "Man, you really are a weak old timer."

"I'm only fifty-seven."

"More than half your life gone. How does that feel?" Philipe instigated.

"About as good as me hitting you with a face-full of chum." Quinn cracked the bucket open. "Want to push me?"

"Easy, Captain. I was just messing with you." "I'm sure that's how you woo all the pants off the guys."

"What are you insinuating?"

"I see how you look at your buddy, Rafael."

"I don't go that way, man."

"Well then, let's get some real man's work done here and maybe I'll believe you." Quinn pulled the lid the rest of the way off the bucket and held it out. "Want a sniff?" "Just slip the coke 2.0 in and let's get this thing back where it needs to be."

"Help me get it on this box here then," Quinn explained as he pressed the top back on.

With both pairs of hands, the two men lifted the ten-quart bucket onto the compartment. Quinn then reached over and opened the compartment next to it and pulled out a little plastic baggie.

"Want a sniff before I dump it?"

"No," Philipe stated. "I don't mince work with my personal life."

"Ah, so you ain't a druggie?"

"No!" Philipe shouted, offended.

"That's commendable. Hell, you could be the poster child for anti-drug use."

"Just put the shit in there!"

Quinn smirked and dumped the bag of drugs into the buckets. He then reached for the ladle that was inside and began to stir it. "My own concoction. Fish heads, innards, and poisoned Coke 2.0." He moaned with satisfaction.

"You're disgusting."

"One has a nose to smell. Why not explore all of them?"

Philipe turned away, deterred by the atrocious odor. It was there he noticed Rafael standing on the opposite side of the dock they were on. His left side was facing them. Philipe followed his gaze and saw he was looking at a group of people getting off a boat. There was obviously tension within the group.

"I take it he was busy scouting for bait?" "Aye, and a long time at that. Why, ya miss him?' Quinn chuckled.

He received a glare from the kid.

"How're your hands?"

"It's only my left hand that bothers me, boy."

"I can easily make it both." Phillip turned and made his way back into the cabin.

Rafael took a puff of his cigarette. He stood sideways, trying not to glare at the group. He did not want to come across as slimy. Even as he caught sight of Ginny, he managed to keep his composure. She was drop-dead gorgeous. Soon, she and the others were no more than ten yards away. He flicked his nicotine into the water and turned to face them.

"Guy's a real jerk, huh?"

"He's not so bad," Patrick stated.

"No, he's worse than that," Maurice snarled.

"I can't begin to imagine how he could have screwed you over. Americans do incredibly well for themselves in the charter business on this island." "Well then you tell him he's missing out." Maurice charged past the shammy looking man.

"What is it he is missing out on?" Rafael inquired.

Ginny tried to grab Maurice's arm and pull him away. Something about the man didn't seem right.

"Who wants to know?"

"Name's Rafael. I'm a skipper on the Bow Dipper."

"Oh yeah?" Maurice approached him, trying to look intimidating. "You hurtin' for business?"

"Most definitely. Now, what is it you fine young Americans want to do?"

"Snorkel!" Josh blurted out.

"Where abouts?"

"Brighten Cove," Maurice grumbled, obviously annoyed at Josh giving away their business.

"Interesting place. Lots of coral formations."

"Yep. It will make for great underwater photography."

"Ah, so you're all filmmakers?"

"Not really," Maurice explained. "We work for a publishing company. Enzo Enterprises. Ever hear of it?" "Sounds like a big business," Rafael chuckled.

"They cover a lot of areas in the market. How does one-hundred-fifty-thousand pesos sound?" Maurice offered.

"Two-hundred thousand pesos, and you've got a deal." "Agreed." Maurice held out his hand.

"You must be eager to get out there. You do realize that's almost six-hundred American dollars, foreigner?"

"The company can cover it. I've wasted enough time on Hank and his mute skipper." "Well then." Rafael took Maurice's hand and shook it vigorously. "Let me just tell the captain and we'll be under way."

"Shouldn't your captain make the deal?" Patrick wondered.

"I handle half of the boat's finances. I can have a good say. A damn good say indeed. Now, let me take your bags and follow me." Rafael scooped up the travel bags and the five made their way to the dinky boat.

"It's a bit small," Josh complained.

"It's got a big cabin."

"Any windows for underwater viewing?" Maurice asked.

"I'm afraid not, señor. We do have a ladder to get in and out of the water with. Hopefully, your camera is waterproof?"

"Top of the line," Patrick said proudly.

A middle-aged man held out a hand for Ginny, who reluctantly took it.

"Ahoy, my name is Captain Quinn."

Patrick stifled a laugh.

"What's so funny, boy?"

"Hopefully we don't run into any great whites out there. Otherwise, you might as well add a T to the end of your name."

"Why?"

Patrick stood silent. He had a hard time believing the man had not seen *Jaws*. "It's a movie comparison." "Media don't do much for me, bucko. The sea is my entertainment."

Rusty watched as the Bow Dipper drove out of the harbor and out to sea. He felt worried. The other two men were not familiar to him and both he and Hank knew of Quinn's shady dealings to an extent. He recalled last night and how he saw some kind of transaction occur.

He hoped there was not any shady activity going on while Patrick and Ginny were aboard.

"It's their problem now," Hank scoffed, turned the key in the ignition and turned to Rusty. "Let's go catch some fish."

CHAPTER ELEVEN

She stood there.

As Sofia Beltran remained stationary in the doorway, she glared at Easi. Her anger was visibly growing. He was ignoring her, watching some noir film from the fifties. The impatience on her face reflected that there was no escaping the incoming argument.

Absorbed in the classical film, he began to suspect he was being watched. He quickly realized that she was standing there. Yet he continued to play it cool, almost uncaring. It was not until she began to tap her foot that his gaze fell upon her.

Her shadow cast down from the doorway as the hallway light beamed behind her. She was beautiful. Easi could tell she was furious, but it did not really bother him. He knew what he was doing, and she just needed to complain.

"What the hell do you think you are doing, huh?" Sofia shouted.

"What's the problem with a little legitimacy?" Easi questioned.

"Legitimacy?" She was taken aback. "You're involving citizens!"

"Tourists disappear all the time in these parts. It's not the safest place for them to be," he explained.

"You just better hope that no one famous gets aboard Quinn's shitty little boat."

"What is the likelihood of that?" he chuckled.

She groaned and then walked towards him. "This operation is at stake. I think it's about time we relocate."

"Perhaps you are right." Easi shrugged. "Or perhaps you're getting cold feet."

She was about to protest but he held up his hand to silence her. "It's not my place to judge. You've been loyal to me all this time. It was only a matter of time until you began to question your place."

"But I…" Sofia started.

"No need to explain. I am a reasonable man."

"I'm not going to abandon you, damnit," she shouted.

"Then what's with all the hubbub? The plan will work. Then after, maybe, we'll look into relocating."

"You're not playing it safe."

"Life's full of risks," Easi grinned. "It's about time I take one."

She laughed. "You act like you're not the biggest risk taker in the region."

"How do you mean?"

"I mean, you basically polluted the water with drugs, made a bunch of dolphins lose their shit, and now you want to poison them to clear any potential evidence of the drug."

"It's a pod."

"What?"

"A bunch of dolphins is called a pod."

"You're unbelievably dense." Sofia turned and stormed out of the room.

Easi turned and looked around the room. The neon light strip above his glowing Coca Cola sign accentuated its popping color scheme. He always found it ironically funny that he had a soda display for that particular brand. It was like an in-joke amongst him and his men. He then looked to his radio. He was in the mood for a good tune and flicked the nob to hear some. *Girls on Film* by Duran Duran began to play. He sat back and enjoyed.

***

The same song played on the radio on the Bow Dipper. Ginny was dancing around to the beat of it. Her gyrating hips were captivating to all aboard. Alongside her was Josh. Patrick was forced to record and endure the torture as the two began to grind against each other.

Maurice was grinning from ear to ear. Patrick took note of how greedy his facial features seemed. His wide smile was distracting, and he appeared to be salivating. He kept wiping his mouth. It was almost too disgusting to glance at.

On the upper deck, Quinn paid attention to the surrounding area. He was hoping the passengers did not have a good sense of geography. The boat was only slightly off course. He would gradually pursue the direction he wanted to go.

Rafael and Philipe were in the cabin below. They were sitting in front of a monitor. Their backs turned to the group, they looked like they were absorbed entirely in whatever they were watching.

"Got the evening news on there?" Josh chuckled.

The two men paid no mind.

"Couple of buzz kills over there," he egged them on.

"Hey, master mullet," Quinn called down to him. "Don't talk to them."

"It can't be that hard to watch for fish," Josh laughed heartily.

Ginny placed a hand on his shoulder and guided him back to the center of the deck. The song was reaching the chorus again and she began to jump up and down excitedly. Patrick continued to ashamedly film her.

There was a familiar thumping sound coming from a mile or so away. With a lack of memory, the great predator associated the sound with food. There was no recollection of what the food had been the last time it had heard the noise. It was symbolic of a meal and that was all it knew.

It changed direction. An overwhelming sense of hunger drove the shark wild. It sped in the direction of the banging when, suddenly, a new sound overcame it.

Eee eee eee eee.

They came from the left, plowing into the fish's body. All four were too fast. Catching them was almost impossible. It had to evade them. As it moved, blood pumped from its gills. The initial attack had proved damaging.

Changing course again, the shark swam further out to sea. The dolphins gave chase. They were not far behind when it swayed its caudal fin sharply to the right. It nearly collided with one of the dolphins. It quickly veered off as the other three continued to pursue.

Turning right, the shark began to circle back. Its mouth was parted slightly as it gained speed. Its whole body suddenly snapped to the right near the three dolphins. Its jaws only managed to chomp down on open water. All three dolphins had darted upward and swam over the great fish.

The trio spun in a circle in unison and then propelled forward, striking the shark, bopping it on the side.

Disoriented, the shark snapped to its right and, again, nearly bit into one of the mammals. Something made it miss its mark. The fourth dolphin had come back and was now nipping at its gills.

With an unnatural speed, the shark maneuvered to its left and bit down on the dolphin's body. Its teeth punctured through the leathery skin. Blood poured upward from the wounds. Then, with all its might, the shark swung forward and tossed the dolphin in front of it.

Making low clicking sounds, the injured animal tried to move. Its whole body was rigid with pain. Looking past the shark, its three siblings were attempting to make a move to rescue their brother.

The shark charged forward. Its jaws swiftly snapped shut, clamping down on its side.

***

A sour expression covered Arnold's face as Rosa and Santos approached him and Loco. He had a sneaking suspicion that today was going to be another awkward day. He did not want it to happen but the way he left the lieutenant detective last night still sat with him the wrong way.

Loco felt nothing from his interaction with Santos. He had no time to waste arguing about it. Instead, he focused on loading the chopper with an automatic weapon of sorts.

"Where did you get that?" Santos inquired.

"You're kidding, right?" Loco chuckled.

"No, I am dead serious. Where did you get that?"

"I know a guy, alright? He gave it to me for a good deal."

"Who is the seller?"

"None of your business."

"I demand to know…"

"You don't demand shit!" Loco spat. "Just because you have a title with the police does not mean you know jack about what is going on, on this island."

"Is that a fact?" Santos chuckled.

"It's an obvious one," Loco sneered.

"Let's just get this show underway," Rosa said, annoyed.

"Yeah, we don't want to wait too long. If we do, we may be here by the time our guns clear customs," Loco laughed loudly.

"Can it, wise ass," Arnold ordered.

"I am just sayin'. You'll be happy I brought this bad boy!" Loco chuckled.

Arnold climbed into the helicopter and situated himself in the pilot's chair. "I don't want to hear any more from you until we're out there." He pointed a finger out towards the ocean.

Loco climbed in next to him and the two started going over the instruments.

"Are you sure these two are capable of pulling this off?" Santos turned to Rosa.

"I hope so. I don't want a fireworks show out there."

"Happy fourth of July," Santos joked half-heartedly.

"Let's go!" Arnold called out to them as he flicked the nob to start the rotor blades.

The two then made their way into the fuselage and buckled themselves in. Unbeknownst to them, there were cases under their feet.

***

The Bow Dipper came to a stop near the shoreline, about six hundred yards out. Quinn wasted no time gathering the supplies needed to carry out the task while the passengers were preoccupied with their activities.

Patrick had noticed something was wrong even through the camera lens. The topography was all wrong. They were not only too close to shore but there was a buoy line running across the area. He carefully zoomed in past Ginny and Josh as they danced. The water looked a bit too shiny. It was as if a rainbow had been cast just above the surface.

Oil slick? he wondered.

"This isn't Brighten Cove!" Maurice shouted up to Quinn.

The captain did not respond.

"Pit stop," Rafael called over to him from the bow.

He was looking out at the water.

"Why does it look like that?" Patrick asked.

"It's an uncommon algae that forms around this area during this part of the year," Rafael explained and then looked at him over his shoulder. "Don't worry. It's perfectly harmless."

"I want to get pictures down there!" Maurice shouted suddenly.

"What?" Philipe asked as he walked out of the cabin.

"Think about it! The rare seaweed would help produce beautiful, natural cinematography."

"We're not snapping photos for a nature documentary," Patrick stated.

"No, but we are aiming to make the front page of the magazine." He turned to Ginny and Josh. "Strap up you two, you're goin' swimming!"

"Uh, what?" Josh asked.

"I don't want to ruin my hair with that shit down there!" Ginny protested.

"If it's harmless to humans, then there won't be any side effects," Maurice explained cheerfully.

"This is just a quick pit stop," Rafael told him.

"I'm not paying for you to run errands," Maurice shouted. "If you want a nice big bonus then I suggest letting us do our work while you three do yours. Honestly, I don't care what you're doing. You should feel the same way."

Quinn looked to Rafael who shrugged.

"Ten minutes down there, tops!" Maurice beamed with excitement.

There was a pause amongst them.

"You get eight minutes and then we're out of here," Rafael said. "With or without you."

"Done deal!" Maurice cheered and then turned to Patrick. "Get the camera ready. You're going down there with them!"

"What about you?" Ginny asked Maurice.

"I'll supervise from above and hand things down if you need them."

The three groaned in response.

***

Hank brought the Sun Chaser up to his and Rusty's favorite spot. It was ten miles offshore. Far enough to see land but not close enough to make out the people on it. Quiet. It was all so silent.

He took his fishing pole and cast it out off the stern. Then he took a seat in his fighting chair and settled into place. The fish usually bit after five minutes or so. Rarely did he get an instant strike. This would give him time to relax.

Rusty came over and began to poke his arm. Hank looked up at him and sensed that something was wrong. His whole frame was rigid with tension. He then raised his hand and pointed towards the port side. He looked to his left.

Squinting, he managed to make out a big, dark shape gliding just beneath the surface. Whatever it was, it was massive. He quickly stood up to get a better look just as twenty inches of dorsal fin rose above the surface.

"Oh my god." It was all Hank could think of saying.

The thirty-two-foot tiger shark glided towards them menacingly. It showed no signs of slowing or changing its course. It appeared to be heading right for them.

"Get the damn engine started, Rusty," Hank spoke as if the wind had been knocked out of him.

The Chinese mechanic swiftly climbed the ladder and turned the key. The engine sputtered but stalled.

The gurgling noise snapped Hank out of his hallucinatory state, and he turned to look up at Rusty. The man was struggling, turning the key, and giving it a few seconds, then trying it again.

"Don't flood it!" Hank quickly ran over to the bow and felt down the dual engines. He examined while searching for anything that would stop the blades from spinning. They were clean.

Suddenly, they roared to life.

"Thank the lord! Get us out of here, man!" Hank said.

Rusty pushed the throttle forward and began to maneuver it in a circle to bring it closer to shore.

The whole vessel then jetted forward and slowly began to go in the opposite direction. Both men fell forward and then back. Rusty landed on the chair hard while Hank began to tumble backwards. He almost fell over the side in between the engines but his calves pressed against the gunwale, and he used all his strength to right himself. He then turned and saw what the problem was. The shark had bitten into the anchor below and was now dragging them away.

With one mighty swing of its tail, it smashed into the glass window under the boat. Water rushed in, immediately flooding the cabin.

"Shit!" Hank screamed. "Get the lifeboat ready! I'm going to cut the anchor loose."

Rusty wasted no time and climbed down the ladder. He then entered the cabin below. A few feet in and he was already up to his waist in seawater.

Producing a knife from the tackle-box, Hank began to cut away at the thick rope that held the anchor. He hoped to buy them a few seconds. Suddenly, the boat slowed and then stopped all together.

Going over towards the bar, Rusty kept his arms up to avoid getting them wet. As he made his way further towards the stern, he brushed against the radio and the song *Maneater* by Daryl Hall and John Oates came on. He paid no mind to the sudden tune and reached for the compartment just below the hatch. A ray of light came down that helped him see what he was doing. The electrical circuitry had been fried from the water intake and the lights were now off.

He opened it and pulled a folded-up lifeboat out of storage. Looking it over, he determined it was usable.

A sudden feeling overcame him. It was not too dissimilar when he saw the shadow of something large swim under the boat from the hull's observation window. He began to feel shivers run up and down his spine. His shoulders tensed and beads of sweat began to spill down his face.

The chorus for the song began and Rusty began to wonder, *Is she coming? The maneater?*

Spinning around to make a mad dash for the entrance, he was greeted with a sight that petrified him in his place. The shadow had returned, along with its teeth.

With grace and ferocity, the tiger shark slammed into the hull and broke through the observation window, further smashing glass and letting more water pour in. The lukewarm salty liquid erupted in frothing madness.

Rusty had fallen flat on his rear and began to slide down to the center of the ship, where *it* was. He desperately reached for anything. Managing to snag the end of the bar, he held on for dear life.

He could hear Hank calling for him. It was hard to pinpoint from where exactly. The whole ship was rocking from side to side. He was surprised Hank even managed to hang on and not fall into the ocean.

Water had already reached his mid-section. It was spraying everywhere. His hands began to slip off the slippery wooden bar stand. The shark's jaws were open wide. A less than inviting invitation.

In an attempt to scream, Rusty flung his head back. His mouth opened and fear and anger were etched on his face.

When his eyes barely parted, he saw Hank over by the hatch. The two stared helplessly at each other.

All the years in Vietnam and their devotion to one another was about to be ripped apart by the ferocious fish.

The tiger shark suddenly lifted its head up and brought it down. The whole vessel began to splinter in two. Rusty was shaken from his grasp and began to slide down.

"No!" Hank screamed for Rusty.

The mechanic attempted to kick at the shark in a desperate attempt for a pathetic last stand. It did not last long. Rusty ended up sliding down the shark's gullet. He was still fighting its insides as he disappeared further and further into the blackness.

"You son of a bitch!" Hank screamed.

The radio crashed into the water, ending the song prematurely.

He then got to his feet and began to run for the edge of the pulpit. When he made it to the end, the whole stern lifted back up, causing the bow to dip into the water. Hank nearly fell off but managed to wrap his arms around the metal railing.

"Shit!" The sudden realization that the shark had gotten free of the Sun Chaser was not lost on him.

He carefully began to shimmy his way back towards the deck near the forward hatch. He tripped over the windlass and fell on one knee. The sharp pain shot through his whole leg. Then, he looked over his shoulder and realized that the anchor was still attached, and it was being pulled further out.

"Not this again," Hank said defiantly.

He quickly reached down for the apparatus and began to cut at the rope. He was briefly thankful that he was cutting rope and not a metal chain.

After a few, excruciatingly long seconds, the line was cut.

Hank began to worry. The Sun Chaser would not be able to take another hit like the one before. He made his way down the gunwale as far as he could. He saw that the lower deck was entirely flooded. He hopped into the water and ascended the ladder, barely able to keep himself from slipping off with each step.

Once he was at the console, he opened the storage compartment beneath it. He grabbed the flare gun and began back down to the lower deck. He made his way into the cabin and over to the bar. Large chunks had been smashed out of it. He hoped one piece would be able to hold him.

He yanked at it. It would not budge. He tried again and again but it would not come loose.

Crack.

The Sun Chaser was slammed into, its fiberglass framing shattered. The shark had broken through the starboard side. Hank looked for a way out. There was none. As the mighty fish broke in further, Hank noticed that there was another piece of loose wood. It was near where Rusty had been taken. It was a thin chunk of the flooring.

The large frame already appeared to be floating when Hank reached down and peeled it back like a large orange. He then attempted to carefully maneuver the object towards the entrance. The shark pressed further and further in. By the time it reached the bar, Hank was outside.

Giving a silent prayer, he leapt off the Sun Chaser and towards the water. His prayer was answered when he and the board beneath did not sink. As soon as he smacked into the water, he dog paddled far enough away to not be sucked down with the ship in a water vortex, and then remained stationary.

Freeing itself, the shark swam around. It was like it was trying to pinpoint exactly where he was and was having trouble.

Hank held his breath as the dorsal fin sinisterly swam by him. It even knocked into the piece of flooring, though it did not pay any mind.

After a few minutes, Hank exhaled but not too loudly. The fish was gone but so was the Sun Chaser and Rusty. He had only two prerogatives now. He had to get to safety and make sure that his former clients were okay.

CHAPTER TWELVE

Crystal Clear.

The plan was simple enough. There was enough clarity below to get sufficient pictures that would look presentable to the publisher. As Ginny and Josh began to motion out further from the Bow Dipper, it became abundantly clear that there was no real danger around. Maurice had a good view of the area. Patrick just hoped he would focus on their safety first and not the job.

Lukewarm seawater brushed past Patrick who slowly lowered himself and the camera into the sea. He was using a Nikon NIKONOS-V. It was the model for the current year and had two lights attached to it. He figured he wouldn't need them but brought them, nevertheless.

There was no chop on the still water. The placid surface would make it all the easier to see above and below. Ginny and Josh placed the goggles over their faces and snorkels in their mouths. They then tread water for a few seconds before diving underneath.

It was like another world.

Under the already glassy surface, the area appeared more enormous than from above. It seemed to stretch for miles before disappearing in a faint haze. Ginny admired everything from the coral reef structure with the arching overhang of rock and barnacles, to the teeming sea life. She saw striped angel fish, a rather shy moray eel, and a few young barracuda that ranged from six to seven inches.

Josh suddenly placed a hand around her waist and pulled her close. She glared at him but saw that he was staring ahead. Patrick was taking their picture while Ginny was awestruck by the sight below. She knew he would not mind but Maurice likely wanted her to remain focused.

Maurice, for all his faults, did keep an eye out for potential danger. After hearing about the dolphins yesterday, he had shown little concern. There was an uneasy feeling about this area in particular though. It was like something was wrong.

Meanwhile, Quinn stood on the bow and began to lower a bag into the water. It was a supply of regular Coke 2.0. The delivery of drugs was planned to be out elsewhere, but they figured it would hold and not get contaminated by the soon-to-be poisoned waters. All Quinn could do now was pray those below would not see the object descending. After a few feet, he cut the rope and let it glide down with all the grace of a rock being tossed into the water.

Rafael and Philipe came up behind him. The former placed a hand on his back as if to say good job. Philipe looked over the side and saw that it had indeed landed right next to the pipe.

"You have good aim," he chuckled.

"There are no currents here. It wasn't that hard."

"What wasn't that hard?" Maurice asked as he finished climbing across the gunwale.

"It's none of your business, sonny," Quinn stated.

There was a tone in there that Maurice did not like.

Both Rafael and Philipe could tell that Maurice wanted to argue.

"How much longer are they going to be down there?" Rafael inquired.

"Five minutes, tops. Then I want to go to Brighten Cove."

"Aye aye, matey," Quinn sneered.

No one had noticed that the bag had not only hit its mark, but a jagged piece of the pipe. It had cut a wide gash and was now spilling into the ocean.

***

The shark's ampullae of Lorenzini picked up something that intrigued it. It was a familiar scent that gave the vague indication of a preferred nourishment. The substance gave off a strong, irresistible odor that permeated the sea like a rotting whale carcass.

Mangled remains of the last meal still clung to its teeth. It shook its massive frame back and forth, focusing its muscles near its head to try and dislodge it. Some of it came out but not all. Limbs were sticking out of its jaws now. It propelled itself forward in search of more nourishment and sustenance.

***

Patrick sensed something was off. Even when looking through the camera, he could feel it. The environment had changed somehow. He kept snapping away at pictures, noticing Ginny inching closer and closer to Josh. At first, Patrick thought it was just for the calendar, a happy couple on a tropical vacation. Then he saw her hand reach for his chest. He fought to not get jealous. This was their job after all.

Her hands found their way up to his neck where she wrapped her entire arm around. She seemed desperate. Patrick was not sure, but he sensed that maybe the environment was turning her on. Then, he realized the truth.

She was afraid.

Following her gaze as she looked down, he too noticed that the coral reef, once teeming with life, was now devoid of it. It was as if all the fish had scattered. No, that was exactly it. Something had scared the fish away which, in turn, frightened Ginny.

Patrick slowly lowered the camera and looked around. Josh gave an expression that screamed annoyance. It was like he was angrily saying *What gives?* That was when he froze in place, Ginny too. They were looking past Patrick who was still scanning the bottom.

The enormous predator came out of the haze. There were human limbs dangling from its mouth as it slowly chewed on them. They opened and shut like some bottom feeder, only partially expanding its jaws.

Ginny had never seen anything so massive before. The fish was as large as a school bus but longer. It was like a freight train with teeth. She immediately wanted to scream but could not muster it, especially because she was underwater. Paralyzed with fear, she just hovered there, clinging to Josh who seemed even more afraid than her.

After what seemed like an eternity, Patrick looked up at them. He was confused for a short while. The look of rigid intensity was not lost on him. He decided something was wrong. They were seeing something that petrified them to their cores. Worst of all, it looked like they were looking past him! He almost did not want to turn around to be greeted by the horrific sight of whatever it was they were gawking at. He decided to get it over with and spun around with his camera and snapped a few shots. Whatever it was would take him but not his legacy.

The shark was mere inches from his face. It sort of hovered there like a submarine but was still propelling itself forward just ever so. It was like it was inspecting Patrick.

It then pushed past him softly and glided around him with a grace that he had never encountered before. The fish would have been a beautiful sight had it not been so large and menacing. With the sun creating dancing arrays of light on its skin, it was mesmerizing. It then began to chew and swallow the limbs that were hanging from its mouth.

Then, it became clear. It was making room for them.

Josh was beginning to panic now, the frozen with fear side of him loosening its grip enough so that he could move. For the first time, he realized how tightly Ginny was pressing into him. Her fingernails were practically digging into his shoulder and back. He managed to pry her off. She quickly curled up into a ball and just sat there. He would not wait around to try and snap her out of it. His fight or flight instinct kicked in. He quickly relinquished the duty of protection and began to make a mad dash for the surface.

No! Patrick screamed in his head.

It was too late. The predator had changed direction and was now darting for Josh. The man was nearly at the surface. He would have to swim a few dozen yards to the boat but, if he paced himself and kept relatively quiet, he would have a chance.

Instead, Josh thrashed around in a desperate attempt to make it to the top. He was only five feet down, but the awkward movements made it take longer than it should have.

The shark began to speed up. Its massive girth moved effortlessly through the water. It closed the gap between it and Josh fast. Ginny and Patrick could only watch in horror as the great predator plowed into Josh with an awesome force. It dragged him down and took his flailing body for a ride. A blood trail quickly formed, bathing the area in red.

Patrick made a mad dash for Ginny who was about ready to scream. He reached out to her, and she shook him off. She was going into a frenzied fit. She was looking out to where the shark was shaking Josh back and forth. Suddenly, his midsection came apart as if he were a loaf of bread and strawberry jelly spilled out onto the ocean floor. She nearly fainted. Patrick tried again to secure her. He placed a hand on her shoulder. This time, she was barely cognizant of her surroundings, and he managed to help her to the surface.

They surfaced.

"Get back in the boat, now!" Maurice cried out.

The Bow Dipper's engine roared to life.

"Hurry,   for   Chrissake!" Patrick carried Ginny, his arm around her waist. It was slow-going but they were nearing the vessel. Then the unthinkable happened. The boat started to drive away.

"What are you doing?" Maurice shouted back at Quinn.

"We need to leave! Pronto!" Quinn yelled back.

"No!" Maurice ran for the ladder. "Wait! I need to get them   aboard!" He felt a sudden sharp pain in his abdomen. Something was twisting around inside his stomach. He looked down and saw a three-inch, hooked blade embedded within. Observing the object, he was surprised how much it hurt. He then looked up to see Rafael staring daggers into his eyes.

"Don't even try." He twisted the knife again, further gutting the producer.

He then shoved him back, causing the blade to take a chunk of meat out in the process.

Maurice landed hard on the deck; blood squirted out in a gaudy fashion. He looked down to see an uncoiled intestine slipping out from the gash. "What have you done to me?" he coughed.

Philipe came out of the cabin. "What the hell's going on?"

His eyes fell upon the profusely bleeding man and his heart raced.

"What's the matter, can't handle a bit of blood?" Rafael chuckled.

"You fucking idiot! He's a producer!"

"I wouldn't care if he were Steven Spielberg. We need to get out of here."

"You've just made things worse."

"Trust me, man. That thing out there doesn't care about our plan."

"What *thing* are you talking about?" Philipe shouted.

Rafael pointed out towards the water. Philipe followed the direction his finger was pointing. At first, he only saw Ginny and Patrick trying to swim after them. Then he saw the gargantuan predator.

"Good lord!"

"Exactly! We need to leave now!" Rafael argued.

"What about him?" Quinn called from above, referring to Maurice.

Rafael walked over to the man who was now coughing up blood. "We'll need something to slow the fish down."

Faster than anyone could react, Rafael grabbed Maurice and began to push him up. Soon, he was half resting on the gunwale and half on the deck. Rafael hoisted the man, nearly dangling him over the starboard side. Blood was spilling into the rod holders.

"This is insane!" Philipe cried out.

Just then, the goliath shark raced towards the boat, past Ginny and Patrick.

"You're an insatiable bitch, ain't ya," Rafael chuckled.

Maurice helplessly watched as the shark's head stuck out of the water. It looked like an oncoming car, just with rows upon rows of serrated teeth. It clamped down on his midsection, biting through flesh and meat with ease. Then, when it was satisfied it had a good grip, it lowered back into the water. He looked down at his mangled stomach.

He turned pale white. Then, he saw a long rope of sorts coming out of him. It was slipping out at an alarming rate.

There was a tug when it ran to its end, then another, then it felt like all his insides were taken out. He was a hollowed husk.

"Fuck me!" Rafael laughed. "The damn shark's got his intestine stuck in its teeth."

"I think I'm going to be sick." Philipe fought back the urge to gag.

Then Maurice was dragged off the boat. He was pulled for a mile before he fell into the sweet release of death.

***

Arnold brought the helicopter along the coastline. It was a steady flight. No strong wind currents or seagulls passing by to complicate the trip. He turned to Rosa who was seated behind Loco's co-pilot seat. She had not spoken to him directly since last night. Things were getting awkward despite him wanting them to be professional.

"See anything down there?" he spoke into his headset.

Santos glanced at him and shrugged while Rosa remained silent.

"What about you, Lieutenant?"

"Are we almost there?" she grumbled.

"You know the area better than I do. You tell me," Arnold said a bit too defensively.

He realized this but was thankful she did not press it.

"Heyo, flybird. Three o' clock," Loco said, pointing.

A mile or so off the shoreline there was a boat. It had been destroyed, the hull cracked presumably beyond repair, and it was listing. The water was deep enough for it to reach the bottom and be fully submerged. The slow process of sinking was the only reason Loco even noticed it.

"It's the Sun Chaser!" Rosa exclaimed.

"Whose boat is that?" Arnold inquired.

"Hank Westin. He co-owns it with his mechanic, Rusty."

"Let's try to hail him." Arnold turned to Loco.

"It looks like the power's out," Santos stated.

Loco tried anyway. "Attention, Sun Chaser, this is Airbus AS350 calling for Hank Westin. Please respond. Over."

They continued to hover there, waiting for a response.

"Hank, please respond. This is Airbus AS350. Rusty, are you there, buddy? Over."

"Rusty's a mute," Santos explained.

"Well shit," Arnold shouted. "Let's scope the area. Maybe we'll find them treading water somewhere."

"What about the plan?" Rosa asked.

"We have two civilians potentially missing. We need to. . ."

"We need to alert the coastguard and continue with the plan," Rosa cut him off.

Arnold glared at her momentarily. He hoped she was not letting last night's disagreement get in the way of her job. It would be very unprofessional if that were the case. "Loco, get them on the horn."

Loco did so and Arnold continued to fly the helicopter along the coastline.

* * *

Hank did not know, nor could he really tell, how far he had drifted. His mind had been racing for half an hour now. The events that had transpired caused him to lose his directional awareness.

The beach was not too far but he dared not try and swim for it. For all he knew, the shark was just below him. The makeshift wooden floor raft was the only thing separating him from the sea and in turn the predator underneath.

Rusty's silent, screaming face kept appearing in his mind. The man had suffered enough during the war. Now, the one place they retreated to for sanctuary was what did him in. He just hoped he was not to be the next victim of that horrible fish.

Splash.

His head snapped over his shoulder. He looked around but did not see anything. Then another sound came in front of him.

Eee eee eee eee.

He turned to see a dolphin staring him in the eyes. He froze with fear. Not only was there a massive killer shark in the area but psycho dolphins.

"Keep away from me!" He shifted on the sheet of splintered wood.

By the sounds around him, he could tell there were at least three dolphins. The other two were behind him. The first suddenly slipped under the surface.

This is it, he thought.

Suddenly, he felt the debris start to move. He began to wonder if they were trying to push him off, though they were not aggressively banging into it. It seemed more like nudging along than anything. Then he began to speed up.

They were bringing him out to sea. He wondered where they were taking him. He lay in silence and began to wonder if the dolphins were working with the shark. He chuckled at that.

Up ahead, Hank recognized one of the houses on the beach. It was Burt's place.

"Why are you bringing me here?"

Then it dawned on him. A couple of miles past Burt's estate was Brighten Cove. They were bringing him there to save Patrick and the others. Something had happened. He just hoped they were okay.

Hank threw his hand forward and pointed. "Hurry!"

A dolphin grumbled in response as if to say *What do you think we are doing?*

CHAPTER THIRTEEN

They did not get far.

As far as Quinn was concerned, leaving now was the only option to stay alive. The two tourists in the water would have to fend for themselves. Rafael did not seem opposed to the idea, but Philipe was having second guesses. He was shaking. Quinn returned his gaze to the sea after looking back at them. The water was still calm and tranquil. It was what was underneath that scared him.

He had no idea sharks could get that big, let alone so aggressive. He had heard horror stories and seen movies. To him, there was no truth in them. All the years out at sea he had never encountered such a ravenous fish. The idea seemed ludicrous. Reports of the dolphins also came to mind. Just what was happening around this island? Nothing made much sense anymore.

The whole plan to involve tourists was ludicrous. Now he had blood on his hands from two of them. Possibly even two more if the other couple did not make it. He wished he had been more vocal. Then again, he did not want to lose his other hand.

Thinking back to Easi and how his little harlot, Sofia, shot his hand, he could not help but get angry. He warned Easi about the potential dangers of the drugs to anyone swimming near them. The dolphins were affected but his employees had been dismissive about it spreading to other animals. The fish was obviously on something, and it was time to own up to it.

The shark was high on Coke 2.0.

"Look out!" Rafael cried.

Quinn's head had been in the clouds when he heard the fearful cry. He looked outward and saw the massive dark shape gliding in front of the boat just under the surface. He steered hard to the left just as the shark finished passing by. Its tail smacked into the hull, splintering some of the fiberglass.

"Shit! We're taking on water," Rafael said, annoyed.

"One more hit like that and it'll capsize us for sure," Quinn stated.

He then pulled on the throttle and brought the boat to a stop. He abandoned the wheel and climbed down the ladder in front of Rafael. The two stared daggers into each other's eyes.

"Can we cut the shit and get this thing out of here?" Philipe pleaded.

"No. I mean, yes, we can put aside our issues. No, we can't go anywhere," Quinn continued. "I made a promise to myself not to die on this trip. To be free of Easi and his contracts. No, I will not give it all up, my livelihood, this boat, to that fish. Despite my name, I won't be sliding down the deck and into the jaws of that shark like Quint. If it comes to that, I'm taking that damn thing with me."

He then stormed towards the toolbox and angrily opened the lock. It opened with a squeaking creaking sound akin to the sound of the boat tilting as she took on water. He fished out a couple of red sticks with some short length of line on the ends.

"Dynamite?" Philipe wondered.

"No shit, Sherlock," Quinn scoffed.

"You want to go dynamite fishing?" Rafael said with a deadpan expression and flat tone.

"Have you any better ideas?"

The three stood in silence. Then, Rafael reached for the toolbox, shut it, and held it at his side. "We'll get your boat good and ready. If you can kill that shark, that'd be great. If not, in the next ten minutes, we're going to leave."

"Done deal." Quinn held out his hand.

Rafael refused to shake it and then turned to Philipe. "Let's get started."

***

"I don't believe it," Loco laughed.

Arnold looked out of the front passenger seat side and saw a figure on a slab of rotted wood. He was moving remarkably fast. "Who is that?"

Rosa looked down. "It's Hank!"

"What's pushing him?" Santos inquired.

"They look like dolphins," Arnold stated.

"What is Westin doing riding with dolphins out here?" Loco asked no one in particular.

"I think they're giving him a free ride." Rosa examined the scene more closely. "It looks like they're heading for Brighten Cove."

Everyone went quiet.

"Okay? What's the big deal with that area?" Loco spoke up.

"Right before it is Burt's estate. That's where the drugs are supposedly being dumped," Rosa said gravely.

"Why are dolphins taking a man to a potential crime scene?" Arnold asked.

"I guess we'll have to follow to find out," Rosa suggested.

***

Ginny clung to Patrick tightly. She did not want to admit how afraid she was or the fact that she was cold. Despite the lukewarm water, she felt she had been drained of blood. Her fear was eating her alive. Patrick held her close as the two treaded water.

The shark had swum by them a handful of times. Each time it maneuvered further away. It was as if it could not decide whether to go after them, the easy meal, or the Bow Dipper, the challenge. There was the sense that it knew they were trapped and would make for easy pickings to come back to.

"Why hasn't it eaten us yet?" Ginny asked. "It's like the damn thing is toying with us."

"Don't think about that. Just stay close to me," Patrick said.

She carefully slid her hand into his and squeezed it. "I want to go steady with you."

"I would not object to that," he smiled.

Just then, the shark changed direction. It was heading right for them.

Patrick began to hyperventilate, and Ginny froze. They were helpless as the maneater began to close the gap between itself and them. Ginny closed her eyes tightly and turned away, burying her face in Patrick's shoulder.

There was a sudden explosion. Water erupted from ten yards behind the shark. A great geyser rose. Water slowly fell back to the sea, gravity pulling it down. Choppy waves rolled over the surface. Some managed to reach Patrick and Ginny and splashed them in the face. When Patrick managed to clear his vision, he saw the shark was gone.

"Ginny, look!" he said.

She dared a peek. Then her whole face came to the sudden realization that the shark was gone. "Where is it?"

Patrick strained his neck to look over the water as they bobbed up and down. He saw Quinn, dynamite and lighter in hand, ready to light another fuse.

The fin quickly reappeared, and he rolled his finger over the flint striker and a small flame produced. He then tossed the explosive over the stern and watched as the water erupted again. This time it was right near the shark's face.

"Hell yeah!" Despite the situation they had put him and Ginny in, Patrick still showed his gratitude towards Quinn.

A faint whirring sound could be heard as the shark rolled on its side. Everyone looked up to see the Airbus AS350 hovering over them.

"This is Arnold Ray," a voice boomed over the speaker. *"On behalf of the Leyenda Police Department, I order you to stay where you are."*

Quinn froze. *Of all the times.*

"We're good to go!" Rafael called up from the cabin. "We won't cross the sea, but we'll make it to shore."

"Did you kill the shark?" Philipe asked.

"Yes! Let's get out of here! The police are airborne!"

"What?" Philipe shouted.

"They're over us right now!" Quinn snapped at him.

The two stayed hidden in the cabin.

"Fucking cowards!" Quinn ran up to the console.

A shot rang out and whizzed past his face.

"I said stay where you are!" it was Arnold's voice.

"Listen, you Texan bastard! The shark's crazy! The dolphins are too! I'm betting they'll be here any moment!" Quinn tried to explain.

He knew it was pointless. They could not hear him. He then mouthed the word *dolphin* in hopes they would at least let them get to shore.

"The dolphins?" Arnold chuckled. "You mean those dolphins?"

Quinn could not see where he was presumably pointing so he looked around. It was there he saw Hank being pulled towards Patrick and Ginny on a makeshift raft by three dolphins. He fell on his rear, laughing.

Above him, in the Airbus, Loco looked at the great fish. He was awestruck. It was like meeting a celebrity animal like Shamu or Bart the Bear. The shark had been mentioned in film and media for years. He always believed it was real when a majority did not. Many claimed it was an elaborate hoax while others said it was possible but not likely.

The thirty-two-foot tiger shark swung its crescent tail back and forth casually. Other than that, and it occasionally parting its jaws to allow water passage through its gills, it remained stationary. It was dying. The local legend of Leyenda, which in of itself meant *legend* in Spanish, was ceasing to live.

"We have to do something," Loco begged.

"We are, we're going to follow the Bow Dipper and get those bastards," Arnold explained.

"No, I mean about the shark."

"Are you crazy?" Santos shouted from the back.

"Well, my name is Loco," he chuckled.

"Oh, let's just get this show underway. Quinn's already through with his laughing fit and is driving the Bow Dipper out of the cove!" Rosa stated.

Loco's brow furrowed. "Arnie, call in a dredging crew or, at least, someone with a strong enough winch to get that beautiful bastard out of there."

"Out of the question," Rosa said. "We don't have time for that."

Arnold reached for the receiver and changed the channel as he began to tail the Bow Dipper. "This is Arnold Rex. I'm here over at the Burt estate near Brighten Cove. We have a massive animal that needs to be transported. Can you send someone out? Over."

"Who is this? Why are you on this frequency? Over," a man's voice demanded.

"Again, this is Arnold Rex. We need assistance in moving a rather large shark. Can you send a boat? Over."

"This is not the coastguard or some fishing boat. We are not responsible for the ocean or its inhabitants. Over," the man explained, irritated.

"My apologies. I must have selected the wrong frequency. Over and out," Arnold said.

Without taking his eyes off the Bow Dipper, he changed the frequency again. Before he could speak into the receiver, Rosa held up her hands. "Wait. What was that last call all about?"

"Just getting familiar with my surroundings," Arnold said, cheekily.

Burt watched the whole scene unfold in his own backyard. It was unbelievable. The shark was massive and now there were people in the water as well as a boat. Above was a white helicopter with a couple of blue streaks on the back sides.

He decided not to call the police. There was already an aircraft there and he assumed the police were involved. Instead, he watched. Then the dynamite went off. Two of them. One landed about ten yards behind the shark while the other exploded right near its face.

Things were wrapping up. Burt had recognized the fishing boat as it had traveled there before. Now it was being chased by the helicopter. He figured everything would sort itself out.

Then he saw a peculiar sight. Three people were being escorted by dolphins to shore. He met them there and helped them onto his property.

"That was quite the show," Burt said.

"I hope the fat lady sang and that that'd be all she wrote," Hank stated.

"There's more?"

Hank looked back over his shoulder. The shark remained still. "It's over."

CHAPTER FOURTEEN

His interest piqued.

The call from the helicopter pilot was fascinating to Easi. The idea of Quinn, Rafael, and Philipe failing the mission had dawned on him. There was no doubt they were, at the very least, being suspected of misconduct. He turned to Sofia who was seething in the chair next to him.

She had been angry before but now she was furious. Things were not going according to plan and all he could do was sit and ponder. The man had been sniffing too much of his own product. He was getting wild ideas.

Easi leaned back in his chair and exhaled. "I think it is time we take care of the ocean."

"You're high."

"No, my dear. You are just not seeing the bigger picture."

"That's what happens when you get high. You think big and make even bigger mistakes," Sofia explained it plainly to him.

Easi ignored her. "Get the car ready."

Sofia's face scrunched up and contorted tightly to create the ultimate angry frown. Easi noticed.

"Now," he said in a demanding tone.

She reluctantly obeyed.

***

A tugboat arrived on the scene at Burt's estate. As they towed in the tiger shark, the crane began to bend but held long enough to secure it to the boat with ropes. The great fish offered very little resistance.

On the shore, Patrick and Ginny looked on with amazement. Hank was spiteful towards the shark for it had killed Rusty. All the while, Burt was becoming bored, indifferent to the whole event.

"Say, since this is my property and the fish died on it, does that make it mine?" Burt wondered aloud.

"I don't see why not," Hank said.

"Interesting." Burt rubbed his chin.

He then walked inside.

"Where's he going?" Patrick wondered.

"Probably to make a few phone calls to the press or somethin' such," Hank chuckled.

The three continued to stare out into the cove.

"I wonder why it was acting so aggressively," Hank stated.

"I don't know," Patrick said. "Maybe it was just a fluke."

"They were dumping something in the water," Ginny said suddenly. "I saw a small pack drifting to the bottom while you were facing away from it, taking pictures of us," Ginny explained.

"Damn drugs," Hank snarled.

There was only momentary silence.

"Where's Rusty?" Patrick asked.

Hank's face tightened. "It got him."

Patrick placed a hand on the older man's back. "I'm sorry."

He fought back the urge to cry, letting a tear slip from his eye.

"He was a good man," Ginny stated.

"The best friend a man could have," Hank's voice quivered.

Just then, Burt walked out and passed the trio. He began to make his way into the water with a camera.

"What are you doing?" Patrick called out to him.

"I   need   proof."
He waded further into the water with his hand holding the camera high above his head.

"You're crazy!" Ginny shouted.

"Let him go. The shark is dead," Hank said through a nasally voice. He wiped his nose.

Some water splashed against Burt's chest. He was deep but not far enough to get a good picture. "Hey!"

The tugboat captain turned in his direction.

"Bring that bitch over here!"

"No can do," he called to him. "We have to get this thing to the mainland for study."

"I just want to take a couple of pictures!"

"Get out of the water, you fool. This area is chum-filled!"

"That shark is on my property! It's mine!"

The man just looked at him. "I'm not sure that's how it works."

"You bet your ass it is! I just want to take a few pictures. Then you can take that smelly bitch away." Reluctantly, the tugboat captain steered the vessel towards the shore while his first mate made sure the ropes were secure.

Burt was soon up close in the shark's personal space. He quickly wielded the camera and aimed it at its face. He snapped away. Flashes from the strobe light illuminated the darkening area. Afternoon was making way for evening.

The shark did not seem agitated, but it was clearly still alive. Even if just barely. Burt decided to risk it and took a few more photographs. This time he backed up a bit to get a wider range of images. He needed scale and locational proof.

"Just one more!" Burt exclaimed.

He then held the camera outstretched and stepped in front of it and the shark.

Click.

In a flash, the shark lunged forward, dragging the towboat with it. Its jaws clamped around Burt's midsection. The teeth dug deep and blood poured out profusely.

"Ah God!" he gurgled.

"Holy shit!" the first mate screamed.

The ropes were loosening as the crane began to give way. The winch began to feed out line and the shark was suddenly free and dragging Burt out of the cove.

"What the hell!" Patrick screamed.

"Where's it going?" Ginny asked.

Hank watched the dorsal fin slip beneath the surface. "To get its fix."

***

A local by the name of Carlos Vasquez had set up the fireworks every year. It had been a tradition for him for over a decade now. This time was different though. He had been requested to do them on the pier. Every time before had been on shore on the beach.

Carlos despised the idea but did not back away from the job. He and a few of his fellow firefighters remained skeptical about the safety of the whole event. Mayor Brunswick insisted that he wanted them to light up the skies far out beyond the pier. *Make the whole ocean glow* was what he had said.

It was a risky business. Still, it was going to be done whether Carlos performed the task or not. They were almost done as it were. There was no need to worry about the set up. It was the payoff that he feared the most.

Near them, a radio blared *Teenage Lobotomy* by the band Ramones as a trio of teenagers gathered around it. They were dressed in punkish garb. They reeked of cigarettes and bad attitudes. There were two boys and one girl. All three were young adults but couldn't care less about their futures.

One of the boys, Dizzy, was headbanging to the tune. "Man, there ain't nothin' wrong with the Ramones."

His girlfriend, Capi, nodded. "Stating the obvious a bit there."

She began to bop her head, her pink mohawk swaying from side to side. She was the only white girl there. Her boyfriend was a local and Turner, the leader of the trio, was from the slums in Mexico. She had a secret crush on him.

It had been going on for a while; the casual smirk or wink he would give melted her heart. She did not really care what Dizzy thought. As far as she was concerned, if she liked someone else, that was her business.

"Let's hit the Ferris wheel," Turner said.

"Ok," Capi chirped up.

"I'll catch up. I'm going to head over to the corndog stand and get some meaty sticks," Dizzy said and looked to Capi who barley even smirked at him.

They separated. The sun was casting a huge orange glow over the water. The rays practically reached them on the pier. Capi thought it was romantic.

"Why don't you dump him?" Turner said flatly.

"What are you talking about?" Capi gave a sly grin.

"You know damn well what I am talking about," he said as they got in line.

"Well, maybe if you weren't trying to be so mysterious about hooking up then I would consider it."

Turner chuckled. "Who said I was being mysterious. I thought I was being blatant."

"Yeah, you kind of were, weren't you," she giggled.

The line moved rather quickly and soon they were in one of the passenger cabins. The two saw Dizzy over by the concession stand and Capi waved.

He looked at them. His face read confusion. Capi figured he would wonder why they had not waited for him. In reality, Dizzy had a plan, and he was determined to see it through. He had suspected the two had feelings for each other and had to be sure.

Turner seemed to notice the vague smirk that crept across Dizzy's face, and he leaned over and kissed Capi on the lips.

"What are you doing?" she asked, shocked.

"Better he finds out the hard way," Turner laughed.

He went in for another kiss. Dizzy was already halfway towards the ride, his corndog forgotten.

"Holy hell! Look at the size of that thing!" Carlos, the firefighter screamed in Spanish.

Dizzy looked over towards where the man was pointing and saw it. His blood ran cold. It was the legend that had come to life. His grandmother had told him stories of the great fish. The striped demon.

***

The Bow Dipper had been chugging along at a slow pace for the past ten minutes. They were not far from the shoreline. Brighten Cove was a mere five miles away. They would not be safe there or anywhere. The Airbus AS350 followed them like a fish followed a chum trail.

Quinn was screaming at the console. He cursed and spat at the controls.

"You piece of junk. Get us out of here!" Shots were fired at them every so often. They were like reminders that, yes, they were being chased.

"It's time for plan B," Rafael called from the cabin below.

"What, do you have an arsenal stashed below or something?" Quinn joked.

"No need to be sarcastic. It will all be over soon," Rafael said.

His voice was quieter. It was almost as if his mind were somewhere else. Quinn wondered what he was up to. Shortly thereafter, he had his answer.

A few well-placed shots hit the helicopter. One hit the rear passenger window, shattering it, while another hit just above the fuselage. Fuel began to leak out.

"Bullseye," Rafael cheered.

"Shit! We have to turn back," Arnold said.

"What? Why?" Rosa asked.

"We're leaking," Arnold said.

"Why didn't we explode if they hit the fuselage?" Santos asked.

"You've seen too many movies. Besides, they hit right above the fuel. It's still spilling out." "Perfect!" Rosa exclaimed. "This is such bullshit. Loco, take them out."

"What?" Loco inquired.

"Eliminate the targets."

"I can't. That would be murder."

"They need to be stopped."

"There are other ways we can handle this, Rosa," Arnold said.

She sat back in her seat and groaned.

"Huffing and puffing won't fix anything. I'll radio the coastguard for a status update. They should have them before nightfall."

As Arnold turned the aircraft to the left, he happened to glance down by the docks. It was there. All thirty-two feet of it. It had survived the explosion.

"My God," he said coldly.

Loco followed his gaze and saw the shark swimming around the pier. It looked as if it were inspecting the structure for a weakness in its stability. The thing was massive. It was over a quarter of the length of the pier. He continued to watch as it swam further out to sea.

"Is it leaving?" Santos called from the back.

His question was answered when the shark charged for the shore. Its directional path brought it straight for the pier.

***

Quinn had seen the shark at the last possible moment. It was when it was a mere fifteen feet from him. Its dorsal fin sliced through the water as its caudal fin swayed back and forth with a speed that drove the shark up to at least twenty-five miles per hour. It was quickly closing the distance to the pier.

"Get us out of here!" Rafael shouted.

"What about the shark?" Quinn asked.

"Go around it!" Rafael demanded.

"I don't know if I can." He steered the Bow Dipper hard to port.

The shark's tail suddenly smacked into the vessel.

"No!" Philipe cried out.

As it started to tilt, the rushing waves brought it about, and the bow began to slip into the water. The boat was going down face first.

At that moment, Quinn could only think of the irony of it all. He always had a bad time when it came to his names. The Bow Dipper and even his own title. He was determined not to let that shark get him.

"Abandon ship!" Quinn hollered.

There was not much time to dwell on the idea of jumping into the water with that thing. The boat was going down whether they wanted it to or not.

Slam.

The shark's cone-shaped head impacted with a solid piling as well as a few less sturdy ones. It made the whole pier shake.

Enraged by the pain, it darted back out to sea. Its tail moved in quick succession for speedier travel. As it passed by the boat it knocked over, its ampullae of Lorenzini detected a new sensation. It was coming from the downed vessel. Not only was there hapless prey in the water but a familiar scent as well.

Plowing into the boat, it searched with its mouth for the source. It felt flesh rip in its jaws, but it did not excite it as much as what it was trying to obtain. Then, it had it. A small bag that was filled with a powdery substance that was slowly leaking out.

Suddenly, a force, a pair of hands, grabbed onto the bag. There was no tug-o-war with the object. The shark simply carried the man out of the wreckage with the bag.

Quinn and Philipe surfaced just as the shark's upper body did. They looked on and saw Rafael climb on its back.

"Let it go!" Philipe cried out.

"The shark wants the pack, man! Ditch it!" Quinn explained.

Rafael could barely make out what they were saying. He felt their eyes on him though. He knew what he was performing was crazy, but it had to be done. "Get me a gun! Does anyone have a gun?"

Philipe felt it was fruitless to find a weapon at this point. The pistol that Sofia had shot his hand with was likely on the ocean floor now. That did not stop Quinn from trying though as he dove towards the sinking Bow Dipper.

The shark's sensory system was in overdrive. The sensations it felt, the smells it inhaled, it was going berserk. With Rafael still attached to its back, it once again charged for the pier.

Rafael fought with all his might to hold on. His right arm was wrapped around the dorsal fin while his left hand gripped the bag. He waited for the opportune moment to pull the bag back whenever the shark parted its jaws. It was all about timing, like playing tug-o-war with a dog and trying to retrieve the toy. You had to be quick and ready to pull.

The lower end of the great fish started bucking up and down. The motion nearly caused him to slip instantaneously. Skin like sandpaper, it began cutting through his jeans. Next would be his leg and then…

He let go of the bag and fell off the shark. When he surfaced, he saw Quinn and Philipe were not too far.

***

Turner saw the fish and what it had done to the boat. The damage done to the pier had also made the whole Ferris wheel shake. It was sturdy enough to withstand the initial hit. Turner could not tell if it would survive another attack though.

He turned to Capi who was panicking and looking around the bushel of people, trying to find Dizzy. Turner then began to hyperventilate. He told himself that if he made it off this ride and back to the parking lot he would try to reconcile with his folks.

Bam.

The same piling had been struck again. There was a splintering sound followed by a sharp creaking noise. The Ferris wheel began to tilt. The framing that held it together buckled under the shifting planks and it suddenly fell through a gap. When it got up to the carts it stopped.

A man flipped over the handlebar and began careening towards the ocean. Instead of splashing in lukewarm water, he landed on a splinter of wood that was stuck, breaking through his spine and stomach. Organs pooled out of his abdomen as he continued to slide down.

If I can get out of here, I'll tell my parents I love them, Turner promised himself. *I'll quit the punk life to go to college.* He then pondered, *Maybe not that last part.*

Just then, the Ferris wheel began to tip towards the surface of the sea. Turner and Capi's cart was first.

"No no no no!" Capi squealed.

"We've got to make a break for it!" Turner explained.

"I'm not swimming all the way to shore with that big fish in there!"

He cupped her chin and looked her in the eyes. "I'll be right by your side."

Capi's tension eased slightly, and she felt a momentary calm come over her. He always had that effect on her.

Turner affectionately kissed her and then helped her climb over the handlebar. "Keep going, I'll be right behind you."

Capi entered the water and then pushed away. She felt naked and alone out in there. Even though most of the area was clear and you could see to the bottom, this section housed a coral bed and algae. She could barely see her feet. "Come on, Turner! Let's go!"

He just sat there.

"Babe, come on!"

"Have a nice swim, you little slut."
"You bastard!"

Turner smirked. "Just get out of here. I don't want that thing coming by here."

With a speed Turner had not expected, Capi swam for him with an agility that he was not prepared for. She gave a shrill scream and then latched onto the bottom of the cart. He wasted no time stepping on her hand with his big black boot.

"Ahhh!" she cried out.

She began to thrash about as he crushed her fingers under his foot. He began to grind back and forth, and she felt some pops.

An explosion of water and a mouth full of serrated teeth engulfed Capi and projected out of the water towards Turner. He tried to jump back but it was too late. With nowhere to go, he felt a white flash of stinging pain in his abdomen. The shark had Capi in its mouth as well as his intestines.

It then began to sink down, pulling a long strand of entrails out as it descended.

Turner wheezed as well as coughed up copious amounts of blood. He had never seen so much blood. Not even when he stuck that old man behind the grocery market last summer. What was even more horrifying to him was that it was his own. His eyes widened, as did the hole in his stomach. Tattered flesh flapped around as his guts rushed out of him.

Then, he was pulled forward and yanked off the cart.

Above, Dizzy began to feel faint. He had watched the whole thing happen. He nearly tripped and fell over the side of the pier when a strong pair of hands grabbed him and pulled him back. He turned to see an older man with a geek and some bimbo. Before he could fully process what had happened, he fell into shock.

***

Carlos held onto the pier for dear life. His massive biceps helped him to maintain a grip with one hand and clutch a fire axe in the other. He watched as the shark knocked the other guy off of itself, then kill those two kids before making its way back out to sea. He knew it was now or never.

He waited momentarily, counting. "Three Mississippi, four Mississippi."

His timing had to be perfect. He did not want to fall when the shark was directly under him or slightly before or after. It had to be precise.

"Ready or not," he let go, "Here I come!"

His descent was graceful as he managed to raise the axe with both hands high over his head. His powerful grip kept it from slipping out of his grasp. Then, with a mighty yell, akin to a roaring lion, he slammed the weapon into the fish, right behind its cranium. Blood rocketed up and splashed his face.

With a quick wipe of the gore to clear his vision, he ripped the axe out and went to drive it in again. He hoped that it would be in the brain this time.

Then, the shark began to move in a familiar way. It was arching its body downward and then up like a bull. He was its rider and would prevail. He quickly motioned for the dorsal fin and grabbed hold. He sat crouched to avoid the skin.

Suddenly, the shark stopped.

"Had enough, aye?" Carlos laughed.

A surge of water overcame him as the shark rolled onto its side. It started turning one-hundred--and-eighty degrees but soon, it was doing full spins. Carlos kept his grip on the fin but could tell it was slipping.

Every time he came up for air he wanted to curse its name. The striped demon, the creature who had haunted the islanders and his grandmother for too long. As soon as he was about to, he would be submerged again.

He raised the axe, one final attempt. Arching his arm back and then extending it. He began to pile drive it down. When it was straight out ahead of him, it slipped and went flying.

Carlos' face froze with fear.

Seemingly in response, the shark dove. Before Carlos could understand what was happening, the behemoth burst from the sea. He and the fish were airborne. The few fingers he had wrapped around the fin loosened and he fell towards the water. He splashed and tried to right himself. A cavernous pair of jaws dove downward on top of him.

Engulfed in darkness, Carlos failed to find space to move. He had been driven down its gullet with the force of being swallowed by a vacuum. Claustrophobia set in. He felt familiar objects like body parts and cans and such. It quickly dawned on him that he too would be trapped in the tummy tomb. Soon, he began to lose his fight with holding his breath and he fell into unconsciousness before drowning.

CHAPTER FIFTEEN

The swirl of rotor blades.

Despite the horror on the pier, many onlookers took immediate notice of the helicopter landing in the center of the parking lot. They saw the pilot, co-pilot, and two backseat passengers climb out of the fuselage. They appeared to be aware that they were being stared at and kept their gazes looking straight ahead. No one said a word.

The shark continued to ram into the pier and yet no one could do anything about it. Four were confirmed dead and one in shock by a random deputy who was patrolling the area when the fish attacked. Hank, Patrick, and Ginny were down there too.

Loco was the first to approach the pier. He soon found himself standing between where it and the parking lot met. He still could not believe he was looking at the local legend he had seen presented in movies and documentaries. The gargantuan goliath pushed itself further into the wreckage, seemingly getting stuck.

Just then, Arnold pointed. "Look! Out there!"

A ways past the pier were Quinn and Philipe. They were towing Rafael towards the shore. The trio looked exhausted, pushing themselves to their limits.

"Let's go make that *arrest*," Arnold nodded to Rosa.

He was obviously referring to her call to murder she had been so eager to dish out earlier. She frowned. "Let's."

She slowly strode towards the beach.

Bang.

A shot rang out. It struck Rosa in the shoulder, and she fell to the ground. Arnold rushed to her aid and Santos and Loco looked for cover.

"Who's shooting?" a random civilian called out to no one in particular.

Another boat, no more than a hundred yards out, sped across the shoreline. It slowed, the engine winding down with a low gurgle. Soon, the vessel pulled up beside the trio in the water.

Santos narrowed his vision to the occupants on the boat. "It's Easi and his bitch!"

"We have to get out there!" Rosa attempted to get up but faltered.

"How? We have no other boat, and our helicopter is leaking fuel!" Loco began to panic.

Rafael was quickly lifted out of the water, followed by Philipe. Quinn began thrashing about. He seemed agitated.

"Are they not going to help that man aboard?" another random bystander asked.

"No," Hank told them as he approached the parking lot with Patrick and Ginny.

"Why not?"

"As per usual, shady shit," Hank responded to the irate local.

"Figures," they replied.

"Rafael! Help me aboard!" Quinn was reaching up.

Philipe wanted to assist but his partner in crime held him back. The two locked eyes He then backed away from the starboard side.

"Consider our contract void, Mr. Quinn," Easi called over his shoulder.

He then pushed the throttle forward and the boat began to propel towards the open ocean. It was with great disappointment by the passengers that it did not get even ten feet. The shark slammed into the hull and the speedboat rocketed out of the water.

Sofia and Philipe fell in immediately. The direct hit resulted in the deck flooding with water almost instantaneously.

The two aboard righted themselves and looked out.

"Swim!" Rafael called to them.

"I'll get the life preserver," Easi said as he opened a compartment.

When he produced it, he quickly tossed it overboard, directly at Sofia. She swam as fast as she could and managed to secure her arms through the hole. Easi began to pull her in feverishly.

"Wait! Let Philipe get ahold of it! We have to bring him in too!" Rafael shouted.

Easi ignored him. Instead, he opted to keep pulling in the line. Sofia's hands soon found the stern near the engines. She reached up as Easi ran to her aid. With one swift yank, he had her aboard. All the while, Rafael was gearing up to toss the life preserver back out towards Philipe.

When he threw it towards his position, it landed a mere five feet from him.

"That's it! Take it!" Rafael pleaded.

He grabbed it and then disappeared below the surface.

"No!" Rafael cried out.

Philipe never came back up. There was no blood. He was just there one moment and then gone the next.

"Blue water!"

"What?" Easi asked after finishing his embrace with Sofia.

"The water's not red! He could still be alright!" Rafael explained.

He then climbed atop the gunwale and dove in. "Goddamned lunatic!" Easi shouted after him.

"Just get us out of here, baby!" Sofia said.

"I can't leave them. They're my two best men!" Easi stated.

"They're replaceable. You're not! You risked too much just by coming out here. It's time to head back and close up shop."

Easi was taken aback slightly by her bold statement. He had been cutthroat but never against his own men. It was a new side he saw of Sofia and he was not sure he liked it.

"Get us out of here," she ordered.

He nodded and ran to the console.

Rafael surfaced just as the boat started to speed off. It was going as fast as it could while taking on water. He prayed they would not make it to land.

Just then, Philipe resurfaced. Next to him was Quinn.

"Gave you two a little scare, huh?" Quinn chuckled.

They then saw the shark break out of its pier entrapment. The front half of it was completely destroyed. Most of it had fallen into the ocean.

"If the shark's still in there, then what hit the boat?" Rafael questioned.

Eee eee eee eee.

A trio of dolphins swam around them in response.

***

"We need a plan to stop this big bastard!" Hank looked around cluelessly.

"We need to get Rosa to a hospital," Arnold shouted to no one in particular.

Everyone looked around, confused and disheveled. Loco seemed to be deep in thought while Santos went to call the sheriff's department.

"I think we can handle this one ourselves." Loco placed a hand on Santos' shoulder.

"Oh?"

"You can call in for help for the injured," Loco continued. "As for the shark, I have an idea. It's crazy. They call me Loco for a reason though." He then ran over to the pier. At the end was the fireworks stand and a few firefighters. They were soaked and afraid. Santos called in dispatch. Afterwards, he thought for a moment. Then it dawned on him. "Holy shit! You really are crazy." He then ran after him.

***

The shark was now on a mission: To destroy everything in its path. There were a few bodies in the water. None were splashing around but it could sense their heartbeats. The ocean was almost void of sea life in its presence besides three familiar mammals. It changed direction towards the shore to avoid running into them.

Pew.

A whistling noise could be heard as an object landed right in front of it.

Kaboom.

A large, cracking noise shook its whole body. A light show occurred in front of it. It was not familiar with this enemy.

***

"Keep firing!" Loco shouted at the firemen.

They were aiming the fireworks down at the water, directly in front of the predator.

"I hope this works!" Santos said, standing next to him.

"It better," Loco said coldly.

The shark raced around the harbor. It seemed to know where the firefighters were aiming and dodged each incoming attack. Even with its massive girth, its speed was impressive.

"I have to give the big bastard that. The thing is quite agile."

"You sound like you admire it?" Santos looked to Loco questioningly.

"If you've been following the exploits of this fish for a while, you too would grow appreciation for it." The fireworks kept shooting past the shark. Loco was becoming increasingly annoyed. After a few more shots that missed the mark entirely, he stormed up to the display and shoved one of the officers out of the way.

"Let me have a crack at this thing."

Taking his time, he carefully pointed the makeshift weapon at the predator. It suddenly started for the open sea. Its tail swept up small waves as it propelled itself forward. Then, it began to dive down.

"Oh no you don't," Loco stated.

Firing at the fish, the firework projectile shot forward in a straight line. It started whizzing around and swirled in an aggressive circle formation until it found its mark directly in the shark's left eye.

Kaboom.

The explosion came swiftly. An eruption of light sprayed everywhere. The shark lifted its head up and shook it from side to side. Its cranium had black streak marks all around.

"Hell yeah!" Santos cheered, as did everyone else.

The parking lot was packed with people. Most were on the pier when it was attacked. Others had driven by and wondered what all the commotion was about.

Patrick and Ginny kissed while Arnold and Rosa embraced.

"Now who's the legend!" Loco mocked the shark.

CHAPTER SIXTEEN

The evening glowed.

As night began to draw closer, *Lights* by Journey played over the ambulance radio. Rosa lay on a gurney. She was helped into the vehicle by a pair of paramedics and Arnold climbed in.

Rosa looked into Arnold's eyes. They showed concern. She felt a weight lifted off her shoulders as well as a sharp pain in her right one. All their arguing and disagreement had not been all for nothing. In that moment, she knew they needed each other.

Arnold cupped a hand on her face. Everything else seemed so distant. All that mattered was Rosa and if she was alright. In his head he lay out their future together. It felt like years when, in reality, it had only been a couple of seconds.

"We got 'em!" Loco cheered as he ran over. "The three in the water. They were hauled in."

"Not that we'll get much out of them," Rosa sighed.

"On the contrary. They're willing to testify and tell us everything," Loco grinned.

"I guess that's what happens when you leave your own men behind," Arnold chuckled.

"Be careful with that!" Hank shouted.

Loco turned and saw the shark being lifted out of the water with a crane. "I better go."

"Watch after your fish."

"Will do, salmon lips," he laughed.

The doors to the ambulance shut and it took off.

Loco stood next to Hank and helped guide the truck driver to get the massive shark onshore in one piece.

"Look at that thing!" Loco bellowed with laughter.

"It's a big boy, alright," Hank said.

"Girl," Patrick said from behind.

"Huh? How can you tell?" Hank asked.

"I not only know my way around a boat, but I also know my fish anatomy," Patrick proclaimed proudly.

"Sounds like a fetish," Loco scoffed.

"It's better to know what you're catching. Females should be put back. That shark is a female. And, by the looks of it, she's pregnant."

"What?" Loco and Hank both turned to him.

Just then, the shark's whole frame moved. Her cloaca opened and a tiny, cone-shaped head popped out.

"Whoa!" Ginny said in surprise.

"Told ya."

The fish slipped out. It began to flop towards the waterline. Loco chased after it while, behind him, two more fish came out. One of them latched onto his leg and, with a sharp twist, snapped it off.

"Ah, fuck!"

A bullet whizzed by his head and found itself embedded in one of the shark's heads.

"Like shooting fish in a barrel," Santos said from off to the side.

The first shark was already almost out to the end of the pier while the one that took Loco's leg entered the water.

"Kill it!" Loco screamed.

Santos fired but it seemed none of them found their mark. The shark swam out, still chomping on Loco's left leg.

"Somebody go get a paramedic!" Santos shouted.

A large snapping sound was heard then. The crane buckled, lines losing their grip around the shark's tail. Loco stared up at the great fish and watched her as she slowly slid back into the sea. For a moment, he could have sworn there was a smirk on her upper mouth. Before he could even say anything, she too was back in the water and he passed out.

Within the next ten minutes, Loco was loaded into an ambulance and carted towards the hospital with Santos in the back with him.

"Wild," Ginny said coldly.

"Now what?" Patrick asked Hank who was staring out at the sea.

"Well, if the shark is still alive, which I doubt, we will be in big trouble. Otherwise, I just have a bad feeling, is all." He then turned and walked away.

Patrick looked out to where Hank was. A trio of dolphins breached, arching their bodies over the sunset on the horizon. *At least part of the sea is on our side,* he thought and then followed Hank with Ginny, their hands intertwined.

***

Within the hour, the offspring found the pipe and the bag and began to swim through the white cloud of Coke 2.0. They retreated when their mother came by. The great fish rammed into a reef bed with an arching formation, smashing it into pieces.

She then rammed into the pipe. Electrical currents zapped her as it cracked, an endless supply of drugs filled the sea. The continuous spillage drove her into a frenzy. Her senses went into overdrive. All she could pick up on was one sound in particular that drove her mad.

Eee eee eee eee.

The End

Check out other great

Sea Monster Novels!

Matt James

SUB-ZERO

The only thing colder than the Antarctic air is the icy chill of death... Off the coast of McMurdo Station, in the frigid waters of the Southern Ocean, a new species of Antarctic octopus is unintentionally discovered. Specialists aboard a state-of-the-art DARPA research vessel aim to apply the animal's "sub-zero venom" to one of their projects: An experimental painkiller designed for soldiers on the front lines. All is going according to plan until the ship is caught in an intense storm. The retrofitted tanker is rocked, and the onboard laboratory is destroyed. Amid the chaos, the lead scientist is infected by a strange virus while conducting the specimen's dissection. The scientist didn't die in the accident. He changed.

Alister Hodge

THE CAVERN

When a sink hole opens up near the Australian outback town of Pintalba, it uncovers a pristine cave system. Sam joins an expedition to explore the subterranean passages as paramedic support, hoping to remain unneeded at base camp. But, when one of the cavers is injured, he must overcome paralysing claustrophobia to dive pitch-black waters and squeeze through the bowels of the earth. Soon he will find there are fates worse than being buried alive, for in the abandoned mines and caves beneath Pintalba, there are ravenous teeth in the dark. As a savage predator targets the group with hideous ferocity, Sam and his friends must fight for their lives if they are ever to see the sun again.

 **SEVERED**PRESS

🐦 @severedpress
f /severedpress

Check out other great

Sea Monster Novels!

Michael Cole

CREATURE OF LAKE SHADOW

It was supposed to be a simple bank robbery. Quick. Clean. Efficient. It was none of those. With police searching for them across the state, a band of criminals hide out in a desolate cabin on the frozen shore of Lake Shadow. Isolated, shrouded in thick forest, and haunted by a mysterious history, they thought it was the perfect place to hide. Tensions mount as they hear strange noises outside. Slain animals are found in the snow. Before long, they realize something is watching them. Something hungry, violent, and not of this world. In their attempt to escape, they found the Creature of Lake Shadow.

C.J. Waller

PREDATOR X

When deep level oil fracking uncovers a vast subterranean sea, a crack team of cavers and scientists are sent down to investigate. Upon their arrival, they disappear without a trace. A second team, including sedimentologist Dr Megan Stoker, are ordered to seek out Alpha Team and report back their findings. But Alpha team are nowhere to be found – instead, they are faced with something unexpected in the depths. Something ancient. Something huge. Something dangerous. Predator X

Check out other great

Sea Monster Novels!

Robert J. Stava

NEPTUNES RECKONING

At the easternmost end of Long Island lies a seaside town known as Montauk. Ground Zero on the Eastern seaboard for all manner of conspiracy theories involving it's hidden Cold War military base, rumors of time-travel experiments and alien visitors... For renowned Naval historian William Vanek it's the where his grandfather's ship went down on a Top Secret mission during WWII code-named "Neptune's Reckoning". Together with Marine Biologist Daniel Cheung and disgraced French underwater explorer Arnaud Navarre, he's about to discover the truth behind the urban legends: a nightmare from beyond space and time that has been reawakened by global warming and toxic dumping, a nightmare the government tried to keep submerged. Neptune's Reckoning. Terror knows no depth

Bestselling collection

DEAD BAIT

A husband hell-bent on revenge hunts a Wereshark... A Russian mail order bride with a fishy secret... Crabs with a collective consciousness... A vampire who transforms into a Candiru... Zombie piranha...Bait that will have you crawling out of your skin and more. Drawing on horror, humor with a helping of dark fantasy and a touch of deviance, these 19 contemporary stories pay homage to the monsters that lurk in the murky waters of our imaginations. If you thought it was safe to go back in the water... Think Again!

www.ingramcontent.com/pod-product-compliance
Lightning Source LLC
Chambersburg PA
CBHW061246170626
46809CB00007B/2870